SQUINT

OTHER BOOKS

BY CHAD MORRIS

Cragbridge Hall, book 1:
The Inventor's Secret

Cragbridge Hall, book 2:
The Avatar Battle

Cragbridge Hall, book 3:
The Impossible Race

BY SHELLY BROWN

Ghostsitter

BY CHAD MORRIS &
SHELLY BROWN

Mustaches for Maddie

SQUINT

CHAD MORRIS & SHELLY BROWN

SHADOW
MOUNTAIN

To Christian, keep being brave.
Between talent and hard work,
you're going places.

Visit us at ShadowMountain.com

This is a work of fiction. Characters and events in this book are products of the authors' imagination or are represented fictitiously.

First printing in hardbound 2018
First printing in paperbound 2019

Library of Congress Cataloging-in-Publication Data
Names: Morris, Chad, author. | Brown, Shelly, 1979– author.
Title: Squint / Chad Morris and Shelly Brown.
Description: Salt Lake City, Utah : Shadow Mountain, [2018] | Summary: Flint Minett has keratoconus, an eye disease, but desperately wants to win a comic book art contest so that he and his new friend McKell Panganiban will be better accepted at middle school.
Identifiers: LCCN 2018018759 | ISBN 9781629724850 (hardbound : alk. paper) | ISBN 9781629726120 (paperbound)
Subjects: | CYAC: Keratoconus—Fiction. | Eye—Diseases—Fiction. | Artists—Fiction | Contests—Fiction | Cartoons and comics—Fiction. | Friendship—Fiction. | Middle schools—Fiction. | Schools—Fiction. | LCGFT: Fiction.
Classification: LCC PZ7.M827248 Sq 2018 | DDC [Fic]—dc23
LC record available at https://lccn.loc.gov/2018018759

Printed in the United States of America
Lake Book Manufacturing, Inc., Melrose Park, IL

10   9   8   7   6   5   4   3   2   1

CHAPTER 1

SQUINT AND ROCK

Double vision stinks. And triple and quadruple vision is even worse.

Sitting at a table in the school commons, I squinted through my thick glasses, trying to see the comic I had been working on for months. The images overlapped, and I had to figure out which was the right one. I blinked hard and rubbed my temple with the eraser end of my pencil.

I had just more than a month until the deadline for Grunger Comics' "Find a New Comic Star" contest. And that isn't much time to write and draw a full twenty-two-page comic. They were going to publish the top five winners online, and the grand-prize winner would get their comic in actual circulation. They probably wouldn't have too many thirteen-year-olds enter. And they probably didn't expect a thirteen-year-old to win.

Clenching my eyes shut for a moment, I took in a deep breath and scratched my head under my shaggy brown hair. "Time to shatter some expectations," I whispered to myself. At home, I may have said it louder, but in the commons at school . . . no way.

I always drew in the commons before school. My grandma dropped me off on her way to her job at the Holiday Inn so I didn't have to take the bus. That put me at school forty-five minutes early, but it was worth it. I hated the bus. I still had to take it home, though. Now it was only about five minutes before the first bell would ring, so a lot of students were filing into school.

I looked down at my drawing.

A teenage superhero and his dog surfed in on what looked like a flying red carpet. Stars streaked past them as they sailed through the night sky and curled around mountain peaks. They dodged a falling boulder just as the mountains opened up to reveal a huge metal castle. They landed at the base of the massive building, the dog leaping off before they stopped. Then in a quick, smooth motion, the red material curled up around the boy's neck. It was his cape, a magical gift from the Empress, and it looked fantastic behind his black outfit.

The boy and his dog slowly approached the

2

massive metal door on the front of a hulking titanium castle. Everything about the building looked thick and impenetrable.

"I should probably sneak in, like a ninja," Squint, the boy in my comic, said.

I had everything he said memorized so I didn't actually have to read the dialogue boxes. That was good. Less stress on my eyes and fewer headaches.

Rock grunted in his low, gravelly voice. Rock was a creature that looked like a bulldog but was made entirely out of rocks. He was, of course, magical as well, forged from magma by the Empress. "But sneaking in isn't your style, is it?" Rock said, sitting down on his tail made of a string of pebbles.

Did I mention Rock could talk?

COMIC RULE: Make your characters unique.

I think a talking rock dog qualifies. Of course, Squint's awesome too. His name was a little weird, but original. His team had started calling him Squint because of the way he narrowed his eyes every time he used his power. Well, his former team. Giving characters strange names, like Squint, is almost a comic rule too. Just ask Ant-Man or Squirrel Girl.

I kept a list of rules I learned in my notebook. That way I

could thumb through my notebook and make sure my work followed them.

But Rock was right. Sneaking around wasn't Squint's style.

Squint narrowed his eyes. In one fluid motion, he pulled both his daggers from their small sheaths on the sides of his belt and jabbed. The daggers were his last gifts from the Empress. Two thick streams of light shot from the short blades. VAROOSH! VAROOSH! They seared through parts of the door, leaving gaping holes with sizzling edges where the thick hinges had been.

Squint twirled one of the daggers in his hand while holding the other at the ready as the remains of the hulking metal door crashed to the ground. KABOOM!

"That was dramatic," Rock said.

"You're just jealous," Squint responded, approaching the gaping doorway.

"Guilty," Rock said, raising a paw. "But now the entire planet knows we're here. And just the two of us going in is a suicide mission."

Squint smiled over his shoulder. "Don't make excuses. You know you want to come."

Rock wagged his stony tongue for a moment, then stretched, his rocks separating a little then bouncing back into their shape. "Of course I do." He ambled over to his master.

Something was off with Rock's leg. I had to tilt my head to see it.

I erased a little of the shading and fixed it. My heart beat faster thinking about how good this story was going to be. And when I won—I mean, if I won—everything would change. I wouldn't just be the crazy kid drawing comics by himself in the commons. People would know who I was. They would all read my comic and ask for autographs and stuff. Taking the bus home would be great, no more Gavin putting his feet on my bench or throwing paper wads or pretending to draw like me, but with his finger up his nose. Lots of girls would want to talk to me, but it might take them a while to get up the courage to do it. And I'd walk right up and say hi to Chloe Williams and she would say hi back. Maybe she'd even get all shy.

It would be the complete opposite of the last time I tried to talk to Chloe. When I heard her group had won a dance contest, I summoned all the courage I had and went to say something to her after class. I walked up to her desk on my way to my seat and said, "Hey, good job on the dance contest." And I rambled a little, like I always do when I'm nervous. "I wasn't there, but I hear you were amazing. I would have come, but my grandparents wouldn't drive me. I'm sure you did so much better than I could. I can't dance to save my life. Sometimes I try and watch myself in the mirror, and it's bad."

She ignored me completely. Well, I think she did. I hadn't talked very loud, and Gavin had cracked a joke next to her, but she didn't even turn my way.

That wasn't going to happen anymore.

CHAPTER 2

THE RULES

Squint and Rock entered a warehouse-sized metal room, which was surprisingly empty. No guards yet.

"I'm not sure that I want to be called Squint anymore," Squint told Rock. "I always wanted to be called something that had to do with my daggers. Like Lightblade or Firefling or The Lightning Kid."

"What about Boy Who Talks Too Much When We Are Supposed To Be Sneaky?" Rock asked.

Squint winked, then yelled into the darkness, "Knock, knock—we have an appointment to save the Oververse!"

Rock shook his stone head.

In answer, at least ten programmed assassin bots

instantly slithered and clanked out of holes. *Chak-a-chak-akk-chk-chk-chk.* Each looked like a robotically enhanced octopus that left a trail of slime as they scrambled toward their prey. On the ends of their legs were guns and spinning razors.

It was an ambush. A slippery, deadly ambush. A present from his former friends.

It hadn't always been just Squint and Rock. Squint had been part of a group of supernatural soldiers, the Five Centurions. Charged with protecting the Empress, they were called Centurions because each of them was worth at least a hundred regular soldiers. But Squint's teammates had betrayed him, kidnapping the Empress they were supposed to keep safe. Squint was here to get her back. And now that he was close, they had sent out the assassin bots.

COMIC RULE: Give your team of superheroes a cool name, like the X-Men, the Justice League, the Avengers, or the Fantastic Four. I thought the Centurions qualified.

COMIC RULE: Give your main character an interesting backstory. If possible, have it include the villains. It heightens the tension.

"That's a rude welcome," Squint said, looking at the approaching bots, then down at Rock. "But I guess I did slice down their huge metal door."

"Not to mention the yelling," Rock said.

Squint shrugged, then narrowed his eyes. The

bots fired first, their shots echoing around the room—
BRATATATAT! In one swift move, Squint jabbed with
one of his daggers while pulling his bulletproof cape in
front of him with his other arm.

The fight was on.

I heard a chair skid across the floor. Not in the comic.
Next to me. "Hey," someone said.

I jumped a little. Nobody ever sat at my table. Plus, I was
pretty wrapped up in the comic just then. Fighting cyborg oc-
topuses . . . octopi . . . (however you say that) . . . is intense.

I looked up at a boy with dark skin, short hair, and shoulders as thick as my legs. He was a little blurry, but I knew who
it was. Gavin. And his new best friend, Travis, was next to him,
taller and thinner than Gavin, with blond hair that reached his
shoulders. They sat down. I covered up my comic with my arm
as my insides rolled. What were they doing here?

But they weren't alone. Chloe, Emma, and another girl I
thought might be in one of my classes followed. Chloe sat,
while the other two stood behind her.

My mouth almost hung open.

The Chloe. Pretty-black-hair-tan-skin-smells-like-coconut-
lotion-popular Chloe sat down at *my* table.

What was going on? Apparently, I had entered some sort
of strange dimension where people like them came to sit with
people like me. A completely alternate reality. What rules of
the universe were going to change next? We lose all gravity?
Students like homework? I mean, Gavin and I used to talk

CHAD MORRIS & SHELLY BROWN

and sit together at lunch, but that was three years ago. Fourth-grade stuff. The rules of the middle-school universe obliterated all of that.

MIDDLE-SCHOOL RULE: Everyone is grouped according to looks, talent, and popularity.

MIDDLE-SCHOOL RULE: Groups don't mix.

My middle-school rules weren't as organized as my comic-book rules, but I wrote them down in the back of the same notebook. Maybe one day I'd make a comic about middle school because innocent elementary students should be warned.

"So Squint, why are you sitting here all by yourself?" Gavin asked, gesturing with one of his thick arms. Squint wasn't just the name of the main character in my comic. It was also my nickname, because I squint a lot. Stupid eyes.

I shrugged, still covering up my comic. Gavin knew the answer. He was just getting in another dig.

"What are you drawing?" Gavin asked, pointing at my paper. Ever since we got to middle school, Gavin had been hanging out with Travis, the tall kid who strutted down the halls like he thought he was a rapper or something. Sure, they were on the football team together, but other than that I didn't know why Gavin would hang out with him.

"My comic," I said, moving my sheets away from them and toward the edge of the table. I wanted to slip the pages into my portfolio case before Gavin and the others looked at them or said anything. My grandma bought the case last year to keep my work safe. It looked like a stiff brown envelope the size of a poster. "You know, my normal stuff." I tried to sound casual, but my thick glasses slid a little farther down my nose, probably because I didn't seem enough like a dork already. I really hated my glasses. They didn't stop my double vision, but they did help with some of the blurriness.

"Oh, interesting," Gavin interrupted, not actually sounding interested. Then he snatched a sheet out of my grasp. Man, he was fast. He looked at it for a second, curling his lip. "We have an appointment to save the Oververse?" he read. That was such a cool line, but he read like it was cheesy dialogue on the back of a cereal box. "And the guy is called Squint? Like you, but he's supposed to be a hero or something?"

I didn't answer.

Gavin laughed and passed it back to Travis.

Travis barely glanced at it. "Weird," he said under his breath and he gave it to Chloe. He didn't even give it a chance.

Weird? My stomach turned not knowing whether to be angry or sick. It wasn't weird. It was amazing. How could they not see it? And now Chloe was looking at it. She would see it, right?

While Chloe held it, Emma and the girl whose name I couldn't remember looked at it over her shoulder. I could see fuzzy versions of Emma's red hair and the other girl's dark, straight hair, but I tried to follow Chloe's eyes.

There wasn't much to follow. After a few seconds, Chloe turned her head toward Emma and said, "Rock dog?" It was like she was asking why we had to do math homework, or why the school served squash with lunch. Like asking why something strange even existed.

I tried to swallow, but it caught in my throat.

"We have a question for you," Gavin said, then looked over at Chloe.

"Oh, yeah," she said, dropping my comic sheet like it was a piece of scratch paper. I snagged it and quickly slid it into my portfolio case.

Safe. I hoped.

If it was even worth keeping safe. Maybe it was better to keep it hidden away.

But Chloe had a question for *me*? Did she want to hang out, or want my number or something? No. That would be crazy. I wasn't in her league. At least not until I won the comic contest.

Chloe moved her black hair behind her ear and leaned in. My heart thudded in my chest.

"Has anyone ever told you that you were cute before?"

Whatever speed my heart had been going before, it quadrupled. No. More like twenty times faster. It was thundering like a stampede of wildebeests. Or like Juggernaut charging an enemy.

MIDDLE-SCHOOL RULE: A pretty girl is one of the most powerful forces in the world. (Every joke is funnier if a pretty girl says it or if a pretty girl laughs at it. Everything she says feels truer. And some people believe pretty girls really have power over time and can make it move in slow motion when they look at you and smile.)

I couldn't freak out. I had to play it cool. Squint in my comic could keep his wits. So could I.

But I couldn't stop thinking, "Whoa. Chloe Williams asked me if anyone had told me I was cute before." The girl that made me look forward to English class.

This was like a movie. The best kind of movie. The kind of movie where the underdog gets the girl.

I tried not to gulp. "Nah," I said, willing my pulse to slow down. My mind filled with other rambling thoughts, but I tried to keep them all in. Cool under pressure. Like Squint the Centurion.

Chloe squinched up her pretty lips. "I didn't think so," she said, and shook her head.

Everything stopped. That wasn't what she was supposed to say. That wasn't what happened in books and in movies.

She didn't *think so*?

She didn't think anyone had called me cute before? Now instead of thudding, my heart didn't know what to do. It almost wouldn't beat. It was like the stampeding wildebeests had all collided with each other. Or Juggernaut tripped and crashed and burned.

Gavin, Travis, and the girls just looked at me for a moment, searching my face. It was way too quiet until Gavin erupted in laughter. Travis, Chloe, and Emma joined him. I couldn't tell if the other girl did or not. I was having a double vision moment.

MIDDLE-SCHOOL RULE: Everyone is always trying to look better than everyone else.

I hated that rule.

"Just kidding," Gavin said, and slapped me on the back, almost knocking my dumb glasses off my nose.

"We thought of it a second ago and we had to try it out," Travis said.

A joke. It was all a setup. How did I not see that coming? Back in elementary, Gavin and I had been on a few football teams together. Gavin was our quarterback. He was really good but always needed attention for it. I was the short wide receiver who could always catch Gavin's crazy throws. He joked then and I dished it back out. He was always teasing. Gavin once told me that his grandma could catch better than I could. I told him I'd be happy to prove that with a little game of catch with his grandma. She never took me up on it.

That was before my eyesight changed. We didn't play anymore. We didn't jab back and forth anymore. It just went one way.

MIDDLE-SCHOOL RULE: Even if you have been friends for most of elementary school, when you go to middle school, if one person's eyes have started going bad and they can't play football anymore, and you live in a town

where football is all that anyone ever talks about, then
that kid with the bad eyes isn't as cool as he used to be
and you don't have to hang out with him. At all.

My chest felt hollow and I wanted them all to go away so
I could scrape my dignity off of the floor and get myself ready
for what was already looking like it was going to be a horribly
long day of school.

Gavin went to slap me on the back again, but decided
against it.

"You have to admit, that was pretty good," Travis said.

I didn't have to admit it, but I gave him a fake smile and
nodded anyway.

Chloe and Emma were still laughing as they walked away.
The girl with the dark hair I think I recognized from science
class smiled as she left. Gavin was the last to turn and point at
me with both his fingers. Like he was so charming or something.

As they left to tell their other friends how funny they were,
I squinted and pulled my comic back out of my portfolio case.
I had to finish it. I had to win the contest. And when I won,
everything would change.

CHAPTER 3

MCKELL

BAZAAM!

I had drawn the word, its letters growing bigger across the page, as Squint sliced through the last of the octopus robots.

Now I was sketching at my table in the lunchroom. Classes had been the usual: blurry boards and teachers talking. Thankfully I hadn't seen Gavin or Travis. The girl who had been hanging out with them really was in my science class. And, of course, Chloe in English. But I couldn't stop thinking about this morning when they had all come to my table.

I ate my peanut butter sandwich on the way to lunch so I could have the whole time to focus on my comic. My table was in the far back corner in an unnoticed alcove. I never had problems getting it to myself because I didn't stop to get anything else to eat. No lines = first choice of tables.

Squint kicked away a robot octopus blade and looked up into the barrel of a bazooka. The huge blaster rested on Gunn's blue-cape-covered beefy shoulder. The bazooka was as thick as a tree and shot basketball-sized spheres of fire. "Why are you here, Squint?"

Gunn took a few steps toward Squint, the bazooka still on his shoulder. Gunn was nearly a head taller than Squint and maybe twice as thick. "Has someone been telling you that you're a hero?" Gunn asked.

No one had called Squint a hero, but he wouldn't fall into this verbal trap.

Gunn had two things he was really good at. One: getting into his opponents' heads and making them lose focus. Two: intimidating others with his really big weapons.

"They don't have to," Squint said, narrowing his eyes.

And then . . . VAROOSH! Squint light-blasted Gavin—I mean Gunn—into a different dimension. Seriously, he was hit so hard and flew so many miles back, he wouldn't remember when he'd last brushed his yellow teeth. Not that he did that much.

Okay. I didn't really draw that last part, but I kind of wanted to.

In comics, I could always think of the perfect thing to say. And if I didn't, I could come back and change it as many times as I wanted to until I liked it. I wished I could do that in real life. I wished I could be clever when Gavin and his friends showed up.

Either that or blast him with light-daggers into a different dimension.

Why hadn't I said something like comic-book Squint would have said? Or maybe when Chloe had asked if any-one told me I was cute before, I could have said, "Yep" or "Definitely." Of course, that would have been a lie, but she wouldn't have known that. Well, unless you count my grandma. Or I could have even said, "Maybe." Any of those answers would have spoiled their joke. Then what would they have done? Looked at each other uncomfortably and left? That would have been so much better.

As I got back to my drawing, the talk in the lunchroom behind me was its usual loud chaos. It almost blended into static for me. Occasionally, I picked out complete sentences as I drew.

"Did you take the math quiz?"

"Can I sit here?"

"Did you hear what Kailey said?"

"That would be so weird."

"Um, can I sit here?"

The noise was easy to ignore. It always had been. Especially now, as Squint had to square off against his former friend. I was shading in his muscles as he pulled out his light-dagger. Of course his muscles were impressive, and bigger than any normal person's muscles. That's a comic rule.

COMIC RULE: All muscles in comics are exaggerated. No hero or heroine has anything but muscle. It's like they only eat brussels sprouts and kale and drink protein shakes while bench-pressing semi trucks and running marathons.

And the closely related rule:

COMIC RULE: Nearly all heroes must wear something skintight so we can see all of their exaggerated muscles.

It's weird, but I go with it.

I started in on a fold in Squint's red cape as I heard more lunchroom chatter.

Wait. Had someone been talking to me? Had someone asked me a question? To sit by me?

I looked up to see a girl with a round face, big eyes, and long dark hair looking at me. The girl from science class. The girl with Gavin and his gang. I still couldn't think of her name.

"Well?" She shrugged her shoulders, her large eyes waiting for an answer. She held a tray with a sub sandwich and a bowl with something green poking out of it.

She must have asked if she could sit with me. "Um . . ." I didn't know what to say. Why was she here? To make another joke?

"Unless you stop me," she said, "I'm sitting." She looked

around quickly then set her tray down and sat on the bench in the corner, hardest to see from the rest of the lunchroom.

Great. I couldn't have someone bothering me, especially not someone like this. Gavin definitely put her up to whatever she was going to do. And I had work to get done. A month wasn't much time if I wanted to finish a full comic.

I slid my pages back into the portfolio, quicker on the draw this time.

She folded open her milk carton, took a sip, then pointed at me. "We're in science class together, but we've never really met." She put her hand out for a handshake.

A handshake? Did anyone do those anymore? I wasn't sure what to do, so I shook it. From the glimpse of color I saw, she had her nails done all nice, like a girl who cares what other people think. If I could trust my double-vision eyes, she had thick dark lashes and was pretty. But of course she was pretty; she was popular.

MIDDLE-SCHOOL RULE: Good looking people are five times more likely to be popular.

"I'm McKell Panganiban," she said.

"Pangan . . . ?" I repeated what I could of her difficult last name.

"It's Filipino," she said.

I nodded. "I'm Flint," I said, "But everyone calls me . . ."

"Squint," she finished. "I know." Everyone knew. For years now only adults had called me Flint. Squint and Flint just sounded too close to each other. And with my eye problems, it had stuck. "I kind of like it," she said. "But can I ask you something about that?"

Here it came. Gavin and the others were probably hiding somewhere close, filming the whole thing on their phones.

I wasn't going to fall into any other traps. I had to be on my guard. "Do you want to know if anyone called me cute before?" I asked.

Ha. Beat her to the punch.

"No," she said. "And that wasn't . . ." She paused, then looked away again. "I don't think that was as funny as they thought." She shook her head, her dark hair swaying. "I mean, it really wasn't funny at all."

I looked at her. Was she saying what I wanted to hear so she could drop a bigger joke on me? Or was she sincere?

No. I couldn't stop to think too much. I had to be confident. Stand up for myself. "Then what did you want to ask?"

"Um." McKell's eyes fell for a second. "I wanted to know *why* they call you Squint. I mean, I asked Emma and she said your eyes weren't that good. Is that it? Because you wear glasses." She pointed at my thick black-framed glasses. "Shouldn't wearing glasses fix it?"

I wasn't expecting that. No one ever asked about my eyes. I don't know if they thought it was too personal or they didn't care. But they never asked.

Wait. Was this a trap? How could she turn this against me?

I couldn't think of anything. Hoping I wasn't about to mess up, I admitted, "I have an eye thing . . . a disease."

But then she didn't say anything. She kind of smiled and listened, like she was waiting for me to say more. No jokes. No laughs.

"It's called *keratoconus*," I said. "It's not like super rare or anything. There may even be someone else in the school with it, but mine is pretty bad. Well, really bad. My corneas are getting thinner and thinner, and that makes my eyes bulge. It's like the windshield of my eye got too weak to hold its shape and now it's shaped kind of like a football instead of a base-ball." I'd heard one of my doctors explain it that way. "It makes everything look a bit like a fun house mirror." I pointed to the ceiling. "Like that lightbulb up there, I see five of them right now and the light is shooting off in weird ways."

If she was going to say something mean, this could be her shot.

But she didn't.

She looked around again, then said, "That sounds pretty awful, but you can see me okay, right?"

"Yeah," I said. "I mean, you're blurry, and sometimes I see two or three of you, but I can see you."

Why was a popular girl asking questions about *me*? That went against all sorts of middle-school rules. She didn't even seem like she was trying to look better than me.

"Thanks for telling me," she said. She pulled out her phone, and then pressed her screen. Was she recording? Or did she just stop recording? Maybe Gavin and the others sent her to get more information about me. Maybe they were planning something bigger.

McKell grabbed her tray and started to get up like she was going to leave, but then looked around and sat back down. I had no idea whether that was good or bad.

"This is going to sound really," she paused, "strange. But can I show you something?"

CHAPTER 4

SOMETHING

Apparently, McKell wasn't done. Maybe this was when she nailed me with some punch line. Maybe instead of recording, she'd been checking her phone so she knew exactly what to say. I wasn't going to walk into it.

"You're right," I said. "That does sound strange."

"Oh," she said and started to grab her tray again.

That wasn't the reaction I expected. Had I hurt her feelings?

No. I couldn't have.

MIDDLE-SCHOOL RULE: What the quiet kid who draws in the corner says never really matters.

But she might really leave. And she was the first person to come sit with me who hadn't made fun of me in the first thirty seconds.

"But strange is okay," I said. "I should know. I'm strange, but okay." What was that even supposed to mean? Sometimes my mouth . . . I shook my head to clear my mind and motioned for her to sit back down. "You can show me . . . whatever you were planning on . . . showing me." I wasn't cut out to talk to people.

McKell took her hands off her tray. "Sorry. I'm just nervous." She brushed her dark hair over her ear, but most of it fell back to where it had been.

I didn't understand why she would be nervous. Popular kids don't have to worry about things like nervousness. "I like to make up rhymes and songs on my uke," she said. "I got challenged to show them to someone. But since I'm not going to bring my uke to school, I'll just show you my rhymes."

"Wait," I said. "What's a uke? It sounds like a hairy animal or something." I pictured her reciting poetry on top of a buffalo thing with bushy fur and thick hooves. "Or is it some cold arctic place?" Doesn't *uke* sound like a freezing, snow-covered place in Antarctica or something? "But that doesn't really fit what you said. So probably not."

Oh, no. More rambling.

"No," she said, laughing a little. "A ukulele. It's like a small guitar."

"Oh," I said. "That makes so much more sense than

performing a song with some huge hairy buffalo, though I would really like to see that. But I wouldn't blame you for not wanting to bring a hairy animal to school."

She laughed again. What I said hadn't turned out so bad. Rock and Squint would be proud.

"So you were challenged to show me some rhymes?" I asked, trying to picture what that was going to be like. I wanted to ask who had challenged her. It was probably Travis or Gavin or someone. This was when the prank was going to hit.

Or not. I still couldn't tell.

"Yeah, rhymes," she said. "Freestyle. Just making it up like . . ." She thought for a moment. "I like rhyming. The timing. The sound, around, the words, you heard." She slipped into it. Like she was writing a poem on the spot.

I blinked a few times. "Whoa," I said. "That was cool. You just made that up?"

"Yeah," she said, her face trying to stop a grin. Her bright white teeth stood out in contrast to her light brown skin.

Usually kids in middle school only write cheesy Valentine's Day–style poetry. That or super mopey depressing stuff. We had a whole poetry section in English class last year and every poem stunk, like skunks-in-a-landfill stunk, mine included. But the rhyming she'd just shared was . . . really good.

"That doesn't seem like stuff you'd say or sing or whatever while strumming a little guitar," I said.

"Oh, it works better than you'd think," she said.

"Do it again," I said.

Another big smile. "Let's see." She thought for a moment. "Mr. Flint, had to squint. For his eyes were not as energized . . ." I tensed. Here it was. She was going to make fun of me. "And McKell had to tell, some rhymes, this time." That was no insult. She had changed the subject away from me to her. "For a challenge . . ." She paused, then bunched up her mouth. "I kind of got myself stuck there. Does anything rhyme with *challenge?*"

I choked on a laugh. Maybe partly because she couldn't think of a rhyme and partly because she hadn't made fun of me. "I'm not sure."

"Ballenge. Callenge, dallenge," she said to herself. She was going through the alphabet just giving the word *challenge* a different first letter.

I couldn't think of anything that rhymed. "It might be a dead end," I said.

She scrunched up her lips to one side of her face. "You're right," she said. "But I think I've bugged you enough. Thanks for letting me do my challenge thing."

That was it? Nothing else? "Okay," I said. I wanted to ask what that was about. Who challenged her to do the rhyming? Why talk to me? Why did she want to know about my eyes? Why had she played with her phone earlier? Had she recorded something?

She looked around, then got up and went over to sit by Chloe, Emma, Gavin, and Travis. But she went a long way to get there. She was trying to make it look like she had been coming from another direction. Like she hadn't been with me.

Was talking to me a secret? Or was she telling them how weird I was? Getting some info for a future joke?

I had no idea.

But I had made her laugh and smile. There had to be some Middle-School Rule about that. I wasn't sure what the rule was, but I kind of liked it.

CHAPTER 5

GRANDMA AND GRANDPA

"You know, Flint," Grandpa said, digging his spoon into his bowl of oatmeal, "back in 2005, Deion Branch, a wide receiver for the New England Patriots, came back from an injury to help get his team to the Super Bowl. And the Super Bowl is the only game as great as," he turned to the University of Nebraska football calendar on the wall, "any game played by our Huskers in Memorial Stadium." He nodded proudly. "Go Big Red," he chanted, almost like he was in the bleachers at a game. Grandpa was a sturdy man with a good-sized gut. And hairy—his hair was long and he had a six-inch brown and gray beard. As short and thin as I was, it was hard to believe I came from the same gene pool. Of course, I couldn't see him that well.

"Do you know what Deion did the night before the big game?" Grandpa asked. Grandpa worked at Jayden's Hardware, but he loved football—with a capital L. He had played in college, helped with the high school team for a few years, and had been a little-league football coach for decades. He had even coached me before my eyes went bad.

GRANDPA RULE: He has a story for everything, and most of them are about football.

"Yep," I said. "You've told me this one before." And that was the only way I would know it. Why else would I care about some old Super Bowl? I spooned more oatmeal into my mouth. Grandma always had it ready in the morning. Or eggs. Or fried potatoes. We had to leave soon.

But my comment didn't stop Grandpa. He was like one of the teachers at school that asks if they've told a story before, but even if they have, they're not going to stop telling it. "Lots of other players were going out gambling, or chasing girls, but not Deion." He moved his spoon around while he spoke.

"I know," I interrupted. "He called all of his coaches to thank them." I figured we should cut to the point.

"That's right," Grandpa said, then turned to Grandma. "See, he does listen."

"But does he?" Grandma asked, raising one eyebrow. She was barely five feet tall, slender, and always wearing makeup. If it wasn't for those times when we went swimming I would swear her face always looked like that.

My grandparents had raised me my whole life. My mom, their daughter, wasn't really good at taking care of herself, let alone another person. And I've never met my dad. So, sixty-year-old "parents" it was.

"The day before the Super Bowl, Deion called his peewee league coaches," Grandpa continued, pointing at me with his spoon, "his high school coaches, his college coaches. He told them 'thank you' for making him work hard, for believing in him, for helping him improve." He set his spoon down and leaned back in his chair. "And then he went out on the field the next day and caught eleven passes." Grandpa mimicked catching a pass. "That was a tie for a Super Bowl record. The Patriots won and he was MVP of the game."

GRANDPA RULE: All of his football stories are longer than they should be.

"Okay," I said, taking another bite. "I get it. He's a great guy."

Grandma looked at Grandpa. "He's not getting it," she said, shaking her head.

Grandpa cleared his throat, pointed at me, then the food, then Grandma.

Oh. I suddenly realized what he meant. "Thanks for breakfast," I said to Grandma.

Grandma laughed and shook her head. "Your sincerity is truly inspiring."

I glanced back over at Grandpa. "Wouldn't it have been a lot shorter if you'd just asked me to say 'thank you'?"

"It would have been a lot shorter if you learned to say 'thank you' in the first place," Grandpa said, his long beard wagging as he spoke. "That's why you've heard that story so often."

I took another bite of breakfast.

"When was the last time you wore your contacts?" Grandma asked.

"I tried to put them in this morning," I said. "But it hurt so bad I took them back out. They're like putting sandpaper on my eyes." I hated my hard contacts so much I only wore them for a few hours every couple of months so that I could tell the doctor that I'd tried and I could pretend that we hadn't wasted my grandparents' money on them.

"Well, thanks for trying," she said. "Try again in a day or two. They're supposed to help." Because my corneas were thin, Grandma was always worried and following up with me. Plus, she was afraid someone would bump into my eyes and bust them. That's why I didn't play sports any more. Well, that and I couldn't see the ball that great even with glasses. Keratoconus really isn't the kind of problem that can be fixed with glasses. But they're better than nothing.

I shoved another spoonful of oatmeal in my mouth, but a weird tingle started in my right eye as I chewed. It wasn't too painful, but it didn't feel good either. I pinched my eye shut.

I'm sure it was because I'd tried to wear my scratchy contacts. But nothing really new. My eyes just hurt sometimes.

"How's school?" Grandpa asked.

"Boring," I said. I never really told them about Gavin or the others. No use bothering them. Plus, Grandpa might go tackle Gavin right in the middle of school and Grandma would call all of their mothers and give them a talking-to. That would be both kind of amazing and kind of terrible at the same time. More terrible than amazing. Except the tackle. That would be more amazing than terrible.

"And the comic?" Grandma asked.

"Really good," I said. "I think I should get it done on time." I made sure not to rub my eye. I didn't want Grandma seeing it irritated. She might freak out. Maybe she'd make me wear goggles to school for protection. Or worse, one of those helmets welders use.

"Did you walk the Hulk yesterday like I asked?" she asked, changing the subject.

"Yep," I said, even though I knew I hadn't. I'd named our bulldog "The Hulk." Both he and the comic-book character are strong and grumpy and gamma-ray monsters.

I'm not sure about the last one, but probably.

Grandma rolled her eyes. "Are you trying to sell me a screen door for my submarine?" That was Grandma's way of saying that she doesn't believe me. Being raised in the South made her hard to understand sometimes.

"Okay," I said, giving in. "I haven't."

"Flint." She let out a full sigh. "You've got to do your share around here or you're going to drive us all into a tizzy."

I didn't say anything. Maybe if I didn't answer, my chore would just kind of fade away. I still had to work on my comic.

"Did you know Coach Tom Osborne had a degree in educational philosophy?" Grandpa asked. "And he used to say—"

"Fine," I said. "I'll do it right after school."

If we were being attacked by a ruthless band of zombie ninjas with death guns, I swear my grandparents would still be concerned about whether I had done my chores or not. Then again, if zombie ninjas were attacking, being with the Hulk wouldn't be a bad idea. Especially if he really was a gamma-ray monster.

The bird clock on the wall chirped Eastern Bluebird. Twelve birds for twelve hours and Eastern Bluebird meant it was 7:00 A.M.

"We'd better go or we'll be late," Grandma said.

Another tingle went through my right eye, this one a little stronger. It hurt, like a pinch. I must have winced because Grandma asked, "Are you okay?"

"Yeah," I said, hoping I wasn't lying.

CHAPTER 6

THE DEAL

I had hoped school would be a little different today, but it wasn't. McKell was in science, but she never looked over at me. Not a big surprise. I wasn't in her league for looks, talent, or popularity. Gavin must have put her up to talking to me at lunch.

Math was okay until my phone buzzed in my pocket. That didn't usually happen. No one from school ever texted me. My grandparents did sometimes, but not during school—I was supposed to be learning. That really only left one person.

I pulled my phone out.

Hey Flinty! A kid at the McD's here looks just like u.

My mom. She texted at the oddest times, about the oddest stuff. My phone vibrated again.

> I mean when u were 5. lol! 😄

I looked at the text for a minute, trying to figure out what I was supposed to do. My mom promised to take me to the movies four times over the last few months and hadn't. She didn't even come for my birthday—and now she sent me this random text? Did she expect me to be happy about it? What did she want me to say? "Wow! Glad you thought of me. You're such a good mom!"

Nope.

I slipped the phone back into my pocket without answering. I didn't want to think about it.

When I got to my table at lunch, I almost jumped. Like one of those I-was-really-startled-and-have-no-body-control jumps. McKell was already there, seated in that same hard-to-see corner and chewing on something from the cafeteria. As far as I could tell, it was a pot pie.

Definitely a surprise.

And she was a brave girl. For eating the pot pie.

Wait. How had she gotten there so fast, especially with lunch? She must have gotten out of class early and been the first in line to be here with her food. That was a lot of work.

"You surprised me," I said.

She grinned. "I could tell." Maybe I *had* jumped a little.

I sat down and put my portfolio beside me. I didn't know whether to pull my comic out with her there or not. Squint and Gunn were in a showdown, but I didn't know how well I could trust McKell.

"Don't you ever eat?" she asked. Before I could answer, she snuck a peek around the alcove like she was looking for someone, or to see if anyone had seen her.

"I had a peanut butter sandwich," I said. "I ate it on the way so I can spend lunchtime drawing." Was this going to be an every day thing?

"How's your comic going?" she asked.

I wasn't sure if she really wanted to know or if it was polite small talk. "Okay," I said, "but I'm behind, so I should get to it." Good one. I turned it into a hint. I didn't completely mind if she wanted to sit with me, unless this was some setup for Gavin and the others. Then I would definitely mind. Either way I needed to get to work, or I'd never win the contest and nothing in middle school would change. I glanced at my portfolio, but still didn't pull anything out.

"Behind for what?" she asked taking another bite of her pot pie. Her dark hair was pulled back in a braid or something.

How much should I tell her? This girl had me so confused. "Well, there's a competition," I said and gave her the basics of the Grunger contest. But I didn't mention how I was going to win and it was going to change everything for me at school, that Chloe would have a crush on me, and no one would bother me anymore. I'd let her figure that part out for herself.

"That's really cool," she said. "When you win, will you give me an autographed copy or something?" With my double vision, I'm not the best at reading people's faces. But she seemed like she meant what she was saying.

I couldn't hold back a grin. "Maybe," I said. My right eye itched a little and I really wanted to scratch it. I didn't, of course.

McKell shuffled in her seat. "Do you think we could make a deal?"

"A deal? About what?" Why would a popular girl want to make a deal with me?

"Well," she said. "I've got another challenge I need to do and I wondered if you could help."

Another one? Part of me wanted her to leave so I could draw. Another part of me wanted to say yes right away. I mean, she was talking to me. She was eating lunch with me. But this was also weird. And maybe even mean. "Who's giving you these challenges?" I asked.

She looked down for a second. "I'll tell you later."

That wasn't a good sign.

McKell took a deep breath. "Will you help?"

I could feel her eyes on me, waiting for an answer. "That's not really a deal," I said. "It's more like a favor. I'm just helping you."

"No," she said. "I haven't finished. What if I help you with your comic, and you help me with my challenge?"

This was getting stranger by the second. And there was a problem. "How would you—" I started.

"Can I look at it?" she interrupted. I saw her glance around the lunchroom again. "I can read it and give you feedback and ideas and stuff."

"No way," I said, holding my portfolio case a little closer and tighter.

"Why not?" she asked.

"Maybe you just want to take it and make fun of it and stuff," I said.

She shook her head. "That wasn't cool when Gavin and the others did that," she said. "I won't. I'll just give you ideas."

"You're going to give me ideas?" I asked. "Do you know anything about comics?"

"Of course," she said. "I've read every Marvel comic ever made." She cracked a smile.

I hadn't ever seen her with a comic. "You're lying," I said. "There's more than 30,000 Marvel comics."

She waved me off. "Yeah, I'm lying," she admitted. "But I do like good stories. And you don't want the contest people being the first ones who read it. Give me a try." She motioned for me to let her see my pages.

I hesitated.

"I promise to treat it well," she said, raising her hand like she was being sworn in at court or something.

She seemed sincere, but my heart started pounding. What if she was a crazy good faker and she was going to run off with my comic book, laughing and telling everyone how stupid it was? But she didn't seem like a faker the last time she'd talked with me at lunch.

She motioned again. "C'mon, I showed you my rhyming, my verse, for better or worse." Another rhyme slipped out. "Don't hold back, and retract, behave brave and attract the pack that will love, the story you're dreaming of."

So cool. Not as cool as comics, but still cool.

I wondered if McKell rhymed for Gavin and Travis and the others. I wouldn't blame her if she didn't. They might tease her like they teased me.

But she was right. She had been brave and it was my turn.

I took a deep breath, reached into my case and pulled out one sheet. Only one sheet. I wasn't *that* trusting. I gave her the panels with Squint facing off against Gunn—light-daggers and a rock dog against a fireball bazooka.

She took it carefully and looked it over.

She put her hands on the side of her head and looked some more.

Did she like it? I couldn't really see any clues on her face as to what she was thinking. Was she going to make fun of it like the others? Shred it? Throw it on the ground?

My pulse was pounding like the marching of an alien army.

CHAPTER 7

DIAMOND

After looking at my comic for much longer than I'd expected, McKell finally said something. "This is good. Really good." And she said it with a smile and a nod. "I think it's cool you named him Squint. Like you." She pointed at me.

"Thanks," I said, hoping I wasn't blushing. But did she mean it? She did have the opposite reaction of Gavin and the others.

She handed the page back. "Can I read some more?"

She hadn't hurt it. She'd read it, said she liked it, and gave it back. She even seemed to be really careful with it. I took in another deep breath and exchanged it with another page.

McKell read it over quietly. It took just as uncomfortably

long as before, then she spoke up again. "Squint is awesome. And Rock rocks!"

KAPOW! She liked it.

Or at least she said the right things.

Maybe my comic was already going to change things.

"But I have an idea," McKell said. She raised a finger with a blue-painted nail.

My heart sank a little. "Really?" She wasn't supposed to have an idea. She was supposed to think that everything was amazing and sit back in awe, relishing my talent.

"Yeah," she said. "It needs a girl." She nodded several times to emphasize her point.

"A girl?"

"Yeah," she said. "Like me." She pointed at herself with both her thumbs.

"Like you?" I asked, suddenly nervous. She probably could tell that I wanted to be like the Squint in my comic. Could she tell that Gunn was like Gavin? And if she could tell, would other people be able to? "Well, there's the Empress." I said. "She's a girl."

"Is she a main character? And does she fight?" McKell asked.

I shook my head. The Empress would only show up on a couple of panels and she wouldn't fight. "But there are a couple of villain girls who will probably fight toward the end of the comic," I said.

"Just villains? Not good enough," McKell said. "You need

a super girl. Someone funny and pretty and her power could be that she can become completely protected, like covered in steel. She's invincible."

"The steel part sounds like Colossus," I said. "That's what he can do."

She looked confused. She definitely hadn't read the 30,000-plus Marvel comics.

"Is Colossus a funny and smart and pretty girl?"

"Definitely not," I said. "He's one of the X-Men, Russian, and has a buzz cut."

"Then it's not the same. But you could change it. Maybe she covers herself in something even more indestructible, like diamond."

A diamond girl. Interesting idea. She'd be really cool looking and near invincible. Wait. It seemed like there had been a comic character kind of like that. But I could make my character a little different. And my comic *could* probably use another girl character.

NEW COMIC-BOOK RULE: It's wise to put a girl in your comic to widen your audience.

"It was a good idea, right?" she said, watching my face. She rested back in her chair and put her arms on the back of her head. She seemed relieved that her suggestion wasn't stupid.

"Not bad," I said.

"Good," she said, leaning forward. "Now you have to go on a hike with me."

CHAD MORRIS & SHELLY BROWN

"What? That's random," I said. "And I never go on hikes."
I could hike, but I didn't really like it. It's the uneven ground.
I'm not great at telling where all the dips and rises are. Hikes
always feel like I'm trying to walk without being able to see my
feet.

"It's not random," she said. "It's my challenge." A smile
flashed at almost the same time I thought she was blinking
away a tear. That's a weird reaction for a hike.

"Why not get Emma or Chloe or someone?" I asked.

She shook her head. "I can't. I'd feel stupid. Just come."
There was pleading in her voice. I wasn't expecting that. No
one really ever pleaded for me to do anything. Teachers told
me to do homework. Grandma and Grandpa told me to do
my chores. Gavin and Travis and the others teased me. But no
one pleaded.

Part of me didn't want to hike with her. "I probably
shouldn't," I said. "I'd miss my bus and have to walk home and
that's like twenty minutes."

"Twenty minutes isn't too bad," she said. "Meet me by the
city library after school."

"Today?" I asked.

She nodded. "I've got to do as many of these challenges as
fast as I—"

"What's going on over here?" A voice interrupted. A voice I
definitely didn't want to hear. I looked up to see Gavin. Emma
was walking with him.

My head almost immediately ached and this time my eye

didn't have anything to do with it. This was the moment they'd been leading up to. All of this had been a setup. McKell was a double agent. She was the Loki to my Thor. I shouldn't have trusted her.

"Why aren't you eating lunch with us?" Emma asked McKell, her long hair done up with some sort of clip.

"Looks like she's found herself a boyfriend," Gavin said and wiggled his eyebrows up and down.

Red. I knew I was turning red. Gavin would even make a joke when one of his friends was setting me up for something worse.

"No," McKell said, "It's not that." But then she didn't say anything else.

Was she flustered? Why? This was the moment everything had been leading to, right?

I waited a little longer, and she looked down at her food. She didn't seem covered in a hard diamond shell. Definitely not invincible.

Maybe she wasn't a double agent. Maybe she hadn't been over here because of them. Maybe she didn't want them to know and now she was busted. That was why she'd kept glancing out at the cafeteria.

"It's nothing like that," I said. "She's tutoring me in science. I'm not that great at it. Mitochondria. Chlorophyll. She's helping me out and earning a little money." I shut my mouth quickly because I could feel myself about to spiral into endless talking and then I'd probably say something stupid.

McKell's eyes widened a little, then she grabbed her tray. Had I helped her, or would she make fun of me for actually trying to cover for her? "So, do you understand mitosis now?" she asked.

I nodded and responded, "I think so. Thanks."

As she took her tray and walked away with Gavin and Emma, she looked over her shoulder. I'm not sure what her expression was, I couldn't really see it, but I'd like to think she was grateful.

I exhaled silently, but long.

It wasn't a joke. She was coming over to eat with me because . . . well, I didn't know. But it wasn't to make fun of me. At least I didn't think so. I couldn't figure out the rules with McKell. Maybe in some ways she broke them.

Now I just had to decide whether I should meet her after school or not.

CHAPTER 8

THE COOLEST THING
IN THE WOODS

"I didn't think you were going to come," McKell said, standing up from under a tall birch tree. The wind blew her hair around a little, but it wasn't nearly as bad as Nebraskan winds can get.

"I wasn't sure you'd be here," I said, walking up to the library with my backpack slung over my shoulders and my portfolio case dangling from my right hand. I hadn't had a chance to talk to McKell again since lunch, so even coming had been a bit of a gamble. I still wasn't sure if I wanted this to happen or not. I mean, she seemed nice enough, but I wasn't going to let my heart pound like a herd of stampeding wildebeests again. There was a chance this could be another disaster.

McKell smiled. "I know this is weird, but thanks for coming with me."

She sounded a little different, maybe more relaxed. I followed her behind the library and we started walking across the parking lot towards a wooded area. She pointed ahead. "We're taking that trail."

I couldn't really see the trail from where I stood. I nodded and followed, telling myself this would turn out fine. It's just a walk on a trail through some trees, not even that far from houses. It wasn't like a hike through the mountains. We don't really have many of those in Nebraska.

But as we walked, I couldn't keep my mind from spinning with the possibilities. Finally, I blurted out, "What are we doing? This isn't leading to some crazy prank is it? Because that's about the last thing I need right now. Are Gavin and Travis going to sneak up and drench me with buckets of water? Or jump out wearing bear costumes and scare the bazaam out of me? I mean, I don't think so after what happened at lunch today, but I'm not sure."

I stopped walking.

She looked back over her shoulder at me, her eyes wide.

I just word-vomited all over the poor girl, and my pulse was racing.

"Maybe I should go," I said, and started to turn back.

"You can't leave," she said, grabbing my shoulder. "We had a deal and I promise there's no prank." She paused. "I don't do that."

I didn't move.

"I mean," she continued, "I know Gavin and Travis and the others would. But that's not me. And all that stuff at lunch today was . . . confusing. I'm kind of new here, just started this year, and I like hanging out with those guys but . . ." She didn't finish. "Sometimes," she started again. She shook her head. "Thanks for covering for me with that science tutoring thing."

I wasn't sure I understood all of what she was trying to say, but I answered the part I did get. "You're welcome," I said.

She gestured me forward. "Can we keep going?"

I thought for a moment, but then surrendered and followed her. Soon the pavement gave way to a dirt trail with trees on both sides. It smelled a bit like a mud puddle. I couldn't see it all perfectly, but I could tell light was scattering through the tree branches and leaves. And by the extreme stillness of everything around us, I was pretty sure that we had entered a different world entirely. Like when Thor landed in Sakaar in *Ragnarok*, but with less garbage and more ferns.

The ground was a little uneven, like I was afraid of, but it wasn't terrible. I managed okay. My portfolio kept hitting random branches that popped up out of nowhere, so I held it to my chest as I walked. I wished we hadn't come straight from school.

"So it isn't Gavin or Travis giving you the challenges?" I asked.

She laughed. "Not even close," she said. "And if they did, I don't know that I'd even listen. Challenges from them would probably have something to do with burping or football." I laughed at that. "Plus, they don't even know I like to rhyme or make up songs, so they couldn't have given me that challenge."

"Really?" I asked. "Why not?"

She shrugged. "I don't know." She took a few more steps. "It's like there are two McKells inside of me." Then she turned it to rhyme. "One wants to be cool at school, to begin to fit in." She took a breath. "But at my peak, I'm more unique. Maybe brave, not enslaved. Just me."

I wasn't sure what all that meant, but it sounded deep. Like she was trying to sort it out herself.

"I have no idea how you can rhyme like that," I said, taking a few more steps.

"It's easy," she said. "You could do it."

"No way."

"Sure," she said. "Just try."

I opened my mouth for a second, but didn't know what to say. "What do I rhyme with?" I asked.

"With whatever," she said, walking beside me. "No. Not *whatever*. That's a hard word to rhyme with." Maybe as hard as the word *challenge*. "Well, I guess you could rhyme it with never, or sever, or lever, or endeavor." Never mind.

"How about I give you a word and you rhyme with it," I suggested. "Show me how it's done."

"Sure," she said.

I looked around. "Brush."

"Rush. Lush. Gush." She was fast.

"Trees."

"Sneeze. Please. Breeze."

"Hill."

"Thrill. Pill. Bill. Chlorophyll." She clapped her hands. "Extra points to McKell for a three-syllable word and a science vocab term. Maybe I really *am* tutoring you in science." She smiled big as we walked a little farther. The sun caught my eye a few times and sent a little surge of pain, but nothing too crazy. It was nice to replace blurry lockers and halls with blurry greens and browns.

"Okay, now it's your turn," McKell said. "Let's start super easy." She thought for a second. "Trail."

"Um . . . pail," I said.

"Good."

I walked for a few more steps, waiting for the next word.

"Good," she repeated and waited.

"Oh, I thought you were telling me good job," I said. "Um . . . hood."

"Nice job."

"Thanks."

"That's not what I meant."

"Oh, uh . . . Spice Bob."

I guess anyone could rhyme. McKell laughed long. "Fantastic."

I thought for a minute. "Uh . . . you got me there," I said, surrendering.

"Elastic," she said. "Or plastic—or drastic."

CHAD MORRIS & SHELLY BROWN

I shook my head. Okay, not everyone could rhyme. "It's just practice," McKell said. "The more you practice, the easier and quicker you can come up with rhymes." She cleared her throat. "If you hear a rhyme, enough times, you rewind, your mind, to that time, and reuse, not confuse or lose or abuse, but repeat the sweet rhyme, different times."

"Whoa." That might have been the longest string of rhymes she had done yet. "That's pretty impressive," I said.

"It's like your drawing," McKell said, walking a little ahead of me. "The more you practice, the better you get."

I nodded. I should be drawing right now instead of trying to rhyme on a hike. Squint and Rock had a score to settle, and maybe I'd try putting in a diamond girl character. But I did have a little more than a month still to the deadline.

"How far are we going?" I asked. We passed a middle-aged couple holding hands going in the opposite direction. That made McKell look around a little. Maybe she was still nervous about being seen hanging out with me. And nobody would believe the science tutor lie out here. "The farther we go, the higher my chance of tripping and falling into a rock and my eyes exploding everywhere."

"Gross," she said. "And you're not serious, right?"

"Not really, but kind of. But mostly not," I rambled. "I just have to be careful." Maybe my grandma's paranoia was getting to me.

"But you could do this, right?" she said, and pointed at a stream near the path. It was only about six inches deep, but too wide to leap across. She started walking carefully from rock to rock. "We're only going a little farther," she said.

I hadn't done anything like this in a while. A long while. But I thought I could do it. And I liked it. I wasn't at home. I wasn't by myself. Maybe there should be a rule about it not being the best thing for a kid to spend most of his life by himself or with his grandparents. "I'll be fine," I told McKell. I stepped onto the first rock. I teetered a bit since I was still holding my portfolio and my backpack, but I managed to find my balance. I had to be careful. If my portfolio fell in, my comic pages would be ruined.

McKell had her backpack on too, but she hopped on the rocks in a way I was never going to be able to. What would it be like to have her depth perception? "We don't have to go too far. I've hiked this with my brother before and he couldn't go very far either."

I didn't know she had a brother. Of course, I didn't know much about her. "How much younger is he than you?" I asked, carefully stepping onto another rock. I pictured a little five-year-old holding her hand as she helped him across the stream.

"Danny?" Her voice caught a little when she spoke. Maybe she was concentrating on her balance too. "Not younger. Older."

Huh. I wasn't expecting that. Maybe he didn't hike far because he was like a *super* lazy teenager.

She went back to hopping from rock to rock. I came up on her slowly but steadily, walking on the same rocks that she did.

On her second-to-last rock, her foot slipped and splashed right into the water. KERTHUNK!

"Oh, no," she said, looking down at her sopping shoe. "I never do that."

I couldn't keep a laugh from sneaking out. "And you were worried about me," I said.

She turned and looked at me, leaning forward. If I could see her eyes better, I bet they'd be pretty intense. "If you weren't . . ." She looked at my portfolio. "Oh, sorry," she said, walking back across the rocks to me. "I should have offered earlier to carry this across for you."

Wow. That was nice. And a change. She had seemed angry for a second. I handed my portfolio to her and she insisted she take my backpack too. Really nice. She had dropped off all my stuff by the time I still had two more rocks to go. She moved faster since she already had one foot wet and didn't have to worry about keeping it dry.

"Your stuff is safe," she said, and turned with a mischievous grin. "But you aren't."

Maybe I shouldn't have laughed at her.

She bent over and scooped some water in her cupped hands and flung it at me.

It splashed me, feeling like liquid ice raining down on me. It was on.

In one good motion, SPLOOOOSH! I kicked a whole spray of water at McKell.

She screamed, getting showered.

She kicked back.

I flung more water.

A few minutes later we were both pretty soaked but on the other side of the stream. And we couldn't stop laughing.

Eventually, I cleaned off the water splotches from my glasses then checked my portfolio. It was fine.

"I want to show you something," McKell said, finally controlling her laughter, and flicking drops of water from her arm. She moved farther away from the stream and stepped over a fallen tree. She held some long skinny branches that would have whipped me in the face if she hadn't held them. After we both passed the branches, she stopped in front of a tall bunch of bushy shrubs growing close together. They all combined into what looked like one giant bush about eight feet tall and eight feet thick. "Want to see the coolest thing in these woods?" McKell asked, gesturing toward the bush.

"A bush?" I asked.

If there were rules about bushes, Rule #1 would be: *Bushes are not cool.*

McKell crouched down and pointed to a small opening in the thick undergrowth. It was just the right size for a medium-sized dog to climb into, the perfect spot for a wild animal home. I didn't want to crouch down just in time to be face to face with an angry badger that wanted to bite off my nose.

But McKell got down on all fours and climbed into the hole. It was the most *Alice in Wonderland* thing I had ever seen anyone do.

I stepped back and tried to look in. Because of the sun outside and the shade inside, I couldn't see much.

McKell poked her head out of the bush. "C'mon in."

I didn't see any badgers.

I tipped my portfolio diagonally and pushed it into the hole. I pushed my backpack in next and then crawled in.

Inside was a room hacked out of the shrub. Or was it natural? Maybe a combination of both. I squinted and saw shoots no thicker than spaghetti weaving their way through thicker branches that formed the plant cave wall. The place was tall enough for a large adult to sit in and wide enough for two more kids.

Ignore whatever I said about bushes not being cool. This place was amazing. Like a little piece of imagination come to life. A great hideout. It belonged in a movie.

McKell sat against the side with her knees pulled to her chest. "Pretty cool, huh?" Her eyes danced a little. Or my vision was bobbing. I couldn't tell for sure. "I found it on a family hike right after we moved here." The sunlight through the green leaves made the whole room speckled green.

"Danny swore this was the coolest thing he had ever seen," McKell said. "And Danny has been in the White House to meet the president, and on the sideline at a Huskers game. So he's been to some pretty cool places."

I was so confused about Danny. He was older than McKell, but couldn't walk very far. He thought a bush was cooler than the White House. Why had he been to the White House in the first place? He didn't exactly sound like a lazy teenager. I tried to think of a question that might help me work this out. "How much older is Danny than you?"

She looked around the plant cave for a moment and took a deep breath. "He's turning seventeen next month," she said. Another breath. "He's the one who gives me the challenges."

I think I grew another wrinkle in my brain. I hadn't seen that one coming. "Why?" I asked.

McKell picked up a branch that had fallen to the ground and started playing with it. "Danny has a YouTube channel. He challenges people to do all sorts of things to make their lives happier. It's called 'Danny's Challenges' and it's pretty popular." She broke her branch in half and fiddled with it some more. "I think it was because it was so popular that I didn't want to do the challenges at first. I mean, Danny's really nice and stuff but I didn't want him telling me how to be happy. He's not my boss or anything." She gave a half chuckle and flicked pieces of dirt with her stick.

"That's how I feel about my grandparents," I said, trying to relate. After all, I had never had any siblings that I knew about but I did know the feeling of not wanting to be bossed around. "But you're doing his challenges now," I pointed out.

She wiped her eyes. I couldn't read her face very well, the light was bad, and my eyes were bad, and my ability to understand teenage girls' emotions was extra bad, but I wondered if she was okay. "I changed my mind. And one of the challenges was to take a friend on a hike, or canoeing, or another adventure." She spread her arms and sniffled lightly. "So here we are."

I was still wet with stream water, sitting in a plant cave with someone I met just a few days ago who seemed like she was crying. It was one of the strangest situations I'd ever been in, but all that was going through my mind was one question: *Did she just say "friend"?*

CHAPTER 9

DANNY

"Flint Keith Minett, you had me as worried as a long-tailed raccoon in a sawmill," Grandma said hugging me tighter than I'd ever wanted. As soon as I walked in the front door, she'd nearly attacked me. "And your eyes are okay?"

I nodded.

I had forgotten to text Grandma to tell her I was walking home and I'd be late. And my phone was on silent in my backpack so I hadn't heard it.

"Is he back?" Grandpa asked from another room.

"Yes." She let go, but sighed in relief.

"I told you he was fine," Grandpa said. I knew he was sitting at the kitchen table with his newspaper and a mug of milk. "Should we eat?" It was only like five-thirty, but that's usually when we ate. Grandpa didn't sound nearly as upset as Grandma.

"I called the school. I made Grandpa drive around looking for you," Grandma scolded, her eyebrows up.

"She did," Grandpa confirmed from the other room. "And Clark let me off the end of my shift so I could do it. Got back a few minutes ago. We were set to go out again if you didn't come home." He must not have driven from the library to our house, because we didn't see each other.

"And that costs us for Grandpa to leave early," Grandma said. "Plus, I imagined the worst things as I drove around." She turned and went into the kitchen.

"I'm sorry," I said, following behind, my shoes squishing a little. My eyes were tired and I just wanted to eat and get some rest. "I wasn't thinking." I felt terrible for forgetting to call. I didn't mean to make her worried.

"What's that sound?" Grandma called out. "Flint, are your shoes wet?" I checked and found a trail of wet footprints. "Don't walk wet shoes through my house. Take those out to the carport to dry."

I had totally forgotten. Thankfully my shirt and pants had dried, but I had forgotten about my shoes. I pulled them off and hurried to the door to the carport. I noticed that there was spaghetti sitting in the middle of the table as I passed through the kitchen to the door. Cooking calms Grandma when she's worried.

"Where were you?" Grandpa asked, scooping up some spaghetti and plopping it on a plate.

"Hiking," I said, dropping my wet shoes. "With a friend."

"Hiking? Where?" Grandma asked.

"On a trail behind the library," I explained, accepting the towel Grandma gave me and pushing it around the kitchen floor with my foot.

"And we had no idea," Grandma said, pointing to a small puddle on the ground I missed. "What if you got lost? What if something happened with your eyes? Flint, you have as much sense as a hen has teeth."

"There were other people hiking there," I defended. "And there were houses not far away."

Grandma continued, "I'm not sure you understand how worried I was."

I reached for my plate, but Grandma ordered me to wash my hands first.

Grandpa cleared his throat. "Who was this friend?" he asked.

"What?" I asked, still a little surprised, sudsing my hands in the sink.

"Who was he?" Grandpa repeated.

"She," I said, rinsing off in the sink. "Her name is McKell."

Almost simultaneously I saw Grandma's mouth turn to a frown and Grandpa's turn to a smile. I know their faces well enough to tell.

"Is she nice?" Grandpa asked.

"Yeah," I said. "She's really nice." I dried my hands off and made my way to the table.

"Are you nice to her?" Grandpa asked, his voice a little sterner.

"Definitely," I said, taking my seat.

He leaned forward. "Always treat women with respect," he said, and then gave the usual Grandpa nod. "Treat everyone with respect, but especially women." He turned to Grandma, "You can continue."

And she did. She continued through most of dinner. She listed all the rules I broke and made some more so this would never happen again. Thankfully, the spaghetti was okay and when I was done, Grandma let me go to my room. I wasn't sure if I was going to be punished or not, or if going to my room was my punishment. They hadn't really addressed that. But I was grateful to escape.

First thing I usually did in my room was pull out a comic. Not today. I'd do that later. I made my way to my old laptop. I closed my eyes, trying to calm down the beginnings of a headache. I'd pushed myself too hard with the hike. Or maybe Grandma had repeated herself too many times.

After a minute, I heard the tune my computer makes when it's finished booting. My fingers typed quickly along the keys: Pangani . . . I didn't know how to spell her last name. I threw in a lot of letters: *Panganifslm*. I hit *enter*. Within seconds, hundreds of hits came up. Most of them were pictures of people from different countries. There was a story about police in Kenya, and apparently Pangan was a place somewhere.

McKell said her name was from the Philippines or India or something, right? Maybe I was on the right trail.

I guess you can't just type in a misspelled version of someone's last name and get exactly what you're looking for. Unless you want random pictures and a story about Kenyan police. What had she said her brother's name was? Danny? And he had a YouTube channel. "Danny's Challenges." I typed in "Pangani Danny's Challenges YouTube."

I hit *enter* and almost instantly stared into a smiling face. A really different smiling face. The boy's head was bald and looked bigger and rounder than any head I'd seen. He had large eyes that seemed too close together. He also had a thin, pointed nose and almost no chin. This couldn't be him. Other than the same skin tone, he didn't look anything like McKell. I clicked back to scroll through the results. But there he was, listed by the YouTube channel, "Danny's Challenges."

Could this boy actually be McKell's brother?

Click.

There was that unique face, smiling as big as his small mouth could, large glasses on his nose, and wearing a Huskers hat that sat oddly on his round head. Danny was at a desk with books and Huskers posters behind him.

"Hello!" Danny said with a wave of a thin arm and hand. His voice was high and squeaky. "And welcome back to another episode of 'Danny's Challenges.'" He spoke quickly and with a lot of inflection. That surprised me a little. For some reason, I thought with the way he looked Danny would speak slower. When he said, "Danny's Challenges," the screen shook and his voice echoed. He obviously put that together in editing. I scanned the details under his video. It had hundreds of thousands of views. And he had 400,000 subscribers? I would have never guessed. What could he possibly say that would get so many people listening to him?

"If you haven't watched this channel before, my name is Danny, and I should apologize for being so much handsomer than you." He pointed and then laughed.

I couldn't help but smile.

"The secret to my good looks?" He leaned in. "It's a genetic disease called progeria. Sorry, but if you weren't born with it, you'll never look as good as me." He clapped and laughed at his own joke. "I always put a link in the description if you want to know more about the disease. There are only like 130 known cases of it in the world. I'm pretty unique." He pointed at himself with both thumbs.

Only 130 known cases? That was way rarer than my keratoconus.

"Here's the deal," Danny continued. "Though I'm a happy, good-looking sixteen-year-old, my body thinks it's a lot older than it is. That's why I have to worry about stuff like heart disease." He pounded his chest over his heart. "It's also why I have this awesome head." He rubbed his bald scalp then winked. "Don't be jealous."

"But," he said, "I'm not as young as I used to be." He imitated an old man grumbling, though with his high squeaky voice it couldn't get very low or gravelly. "I haven't been feeling great. I'm on some extra medications, etc. Boring stuff." The video cut to Danny snoring. Then it cut to the next scene and he was awake. "The bottom line is that I want you to go out and do what I can't right now."

He pointed both of his thin index fingers at me through the screen. "Your challenge this week is to go outside on an adventure. Explore a swamp. Climb a mountain, canoe across a lake . . . do something outside. Go somewhere I would want to go." The screen flashed with pictures of him in the outdoors, canoeing on a lake, rappelling off a mountainside, hiking with a light backpack. "It doesn't have to be a big deal. Those who know me well, know that my muscles can't take me as far or as fast as others, but I still love it. For example, I love to do a simple little hike with my sister really close to our house that ends in this awesome secret place."

Yep. This was definitely the right guy. And McKell had brought me to that place. I felt kind of flattered.

The camera zoomed in on Danny. "Got a place in mind?" He paused for a moment as if waiting for the listener to say something. "Good. But there is one more catch to the challenge, you have to bring at least one other person along. It's always more fun with someone else. Take a friend. Meet a new friend. Take someone with you." The camera came in for a close-up and he wiggled his eyebrows. "Uh huh," he said.

"Maybe even someone you kind of like. Or someone you want to find out if you kind of like." The camera zoomed back out. "Or someone who's lonely. Or someone you want to meet. I would want to meet them all, and I'd go with you if I could."

Wait. Which category was I in? McKell only said a friend. She didn't kind of like me, did she? Or maybe I was someone who looked lonely. That seemed much more likely.

"So go out there and explore. Climb, hike, adventure. Climb something. Wait. Did I say climb twice?" Why didn't Danny edit out his mistake? I would have. I mean, I edit my comics until I have them the way I want them. "Go somewhere I would go."

Danny seemed like a great guy. A little weird, and definitely different looking, but a good guy.

I clicked on another video. Danny was even more energetic. I watched several videos, clicking on whichever one came up in the playlist next. He challenged people to read a book, to listen to a whole album of music they had never listened to before, to be nicer to their moms, to go a whole week without desserts—all sorts of things. There was a decent amount of variety to his challenges. I clicked on another.

Danny talked about how he wanted to make lots of friends and be with people, but sometimes he didn't have the energy. "But there is always a way to do what you really want," he said. Then he shared about making his YouTube channel. He said he was really nervous to show it to others. But he said that a friend named Yellow saw it, was super supportive and helped him edit it. I have no idea what kind of a name Yellow was, but at least he was helping out in a good cause. "So share something you create with someone else. I share my videos. Maybe you write cool songs and rhymes like my sister. Maybe you take amazing pictures. Maybe you draw. I know you have a talent. Use it and share it." He bobbed his eyebrows up and down. "Use it and share it," he repeated.

My mind immediately jumped to my drawings. Other than my grandma and grandpa, McKell was really the only one that had seen them. I had kind of already done that one with her. But I was in no hurry to let anyone else look at them. I didn't want anyone else making fun of them. Not Gavin. Not Travis. No one. Well, I guess I'd have to let the contest judges see them.

But this challenge would explain why McKell shared her rhyming with me. Maybe when she was messing with her phone she wasn't recording anything but checking her list of challenges.

I clicked the *subscribe* button. I'd watch one more before getting back to Squint and his quest to save the Empress. I clicked the next video.

"Hey, world," Danny said and jumped into one of his usual intros. "Here's a story for today," he said. "When I first moved to Lincoln, I was pretty out of place. Plus, I don't know if you'd believe this or not, but some people couldn't stop staring at my beautiful face." He framed his face with his hands. "I ate lunch alone. I hated it. I wanted so badly to be with people.

To laugh, to joke, to hang out. But none of them gave me a chance at first." He took a breath. "So I decided to help them along. I looked for someone who looked lonely and I went and sat with them. And that turned out to be one of the best things I've ever done. It put me on a path to make some great friends."

That sounded hard. I mean, I figured that nobody wanted to eat lunch with me—that's why nobody did. If I went and sat with others I could only imagine that going badly.

Danny pointed at the camera again. "Your turn. Find someone at school, or work, or wherever. Maybe they look lonely. Maybe they don't have any friends. Introduce yourself. Sit with them. Get to know them. That is your challenge for the day."

Could I do it?

Wait.

That's what McKell was doing. I was the lonely kid. That was why she ate part of lunch with me in the first place.

Maybe I wasn't a friend.

Maybe I was just a challenge.

CHAPTER 10

TORN

"Flint!" A shrill voice rang from down the hall. Sometimes Grandma's voice was all singsongy, but not now.

"Flint!"

A tingling feeling started at the front of my right eye and streamed behind it. Apparently, my grandma's voice was actually breaking things inside of me. I always suspected as much. Or maybe my eye was extra irritated today. I don't know if it was those awful contacts or going on that hike.

"You need to answer me." Grandma stepped into the doorway. I could see her big blonde hair and blue jeans.

I looked up. "Hey, Grandma." I tried to sound like I had barely heard her for the first time.

"Do you have rocks in your ears?" she asked.

"No," I said. "Sorry, I was looking something up."

She softened a little. "You didn't walk the Hulk, did you?" she asked.

"Sorry," I said. "I meant to, it's just that—"

"So," Grandma interrupted, "this is when you show that you're sorry by running out there and taking care of it." She only waited a moment.

I got up out of my chair and passed her before wiping my weepy eye. No use getting her worried.

I found the Hulk in the brush outside of Grandma's flower bed, the moving mound of brown fur among all the other colors. "Hey, Hulk," I said, and lowered my voice. "Come here, I've got a . . . job for you." I tried to sound like Batman or something. Real tough. It was the same way Squint would talk to Rock.

I caught the Hulk around the back and belly, then worked my hands up to the loop on his collar to hook on the leash. I tried not to get too close to his mouth. His Hulk breath smelled worse than the boys' locker room. That's definitely a downside to the gamma rays that they never mention in the comic books.

Blinding light hit me and immediately my eye stung. Stupid sun—right in my eyes.

It took a couple of seconds to recover, but then we set off. I passed our neighbors, the family from Italy. At least I think they were. Something like that. What was their last name?

Grandma said it all the time. The dad was working on a car he had parked in the street.

"Hey, Flint," he said. Adults usually call me by my real name. But what was his name? Marco? Marcello? Milano?

I nodded and let out a mumble that meant hello. Why did people say hello when passing each other? Most people don't stop to talk and I'm fine with that.

"Well," he said, realizing I wasn't going to say anything else, "it was good catching up with you, too." He chuckled as he leaned back in over the car. He did like to laugh, especially at his own jokes.

Wow, the sun was bright. I felt like I stood under some massive vaporizing laser. Of course having the light go through my thick glasses didn't help. The glare lingered. I had to blink a few extra times and shaded my eyes. Or maybe it was bugging me so badly because I had that headache coming on. I could already feel the throbbing start behind my right eye.

The Hulk stopped his stubbly waddle to sniff the base of a tree. He slobbered a little on it too. "Come on, boy," I said and tugged on the leash. "Remember that job you've got to do." Again, I used my Batman voice.

My right eye pulsed. I wiped it under my glasses with my sleeve. It was full on watering now.

Why did it still seem bright even with my eye closed?

Pain.

Real pain.

All through my eye.

I stopped. The Hulk yanked at the leash. "Stop it," I said, my voice short and sharp. No more Batman voice. I wasn't playing. "Let's go back."

I turned and started back with my hand cupped over one side of my glasses and my eye. The Hulk ran back the other way, pulling on the leash and letting out short, happy, but demanding barks. He definitely wanted a full walk. I tugged back hard. I had to get inside.

"Ahhh!" I almost dropped the leash. The pain surged so much I almost didn't realize that I let the scream out. I faltered and fell to one knee onto the cement. I covered my eye with the other hand as well. The Hulk licked my face. I pushed him back.

"Ahhh!" I let out again.

"Are you okay?" A deep voice asked.

"My eye is killing me," I said without thinking.

"How can I help?" he asked. It was Marco, or whatever his name was.

I didn't answer.

"Can you walk?"

I nodded and I stood while the pain faded a little. But I knew the next wave would hit soon. A strong arm reached around my back and under my arm. It smelled like grease and sweat, but I didn't care.

"Ahhh!" My eye was nearly on fire.

Those strong arms scooped me up and Marco started to run.

CHAPTER 11

PATCH

I would have rather faced Galactus trying to devour my entire planet than go back to school, but six days after the eye incident I moved down the hall toward my next class. Six days of rest and headaches. Turns out the sun hadn't really been brighter. My cornea, the thin outside layer of my eye, had torn. My wonky windshield broke. Now I had to keep it covered and put eye drops in every few hours until I could have some terrifying surgery to fix it. I tried not to think about it.

"Whoa!" Gavin came at me head-on and grabbed me by the shoulders. Others in the crowded halls passed us. "Look who we have here." He closed one eye, put up a bent pointer finger, and used his best pirate voice. "It be Squint. And he be squintin'. Arrr."

It was the eye patch. Yep. I was a seventh grader walking the halls of middle school wearing an eye patch under my glasses. Doctor's orders and Grandma's nonnegotiable commands. I still had to wear my glasses because my other eye needed them to see anything.

MIDDLE-SCHOOL RULE: If there is an easy joke, someone will take it. (And a boy wearing an eye patch under his glasses is definitely an easy joke.)

At first, I kind of liked the eye patch. I felt like Nick Fury, the bald guy who led the Avengers and S.H.I.E.L.D. But then I tried to draw and it was even harder than before. I guess it made sense; I could only look through one of my kind-of-broken eyes. I was down to under a month to finish my comic and it was more difficult than ever.

"The glasses over the patch just isn't working," Travis said, then turned to Gavin. "It's like he's trying to look tough, but can't quite pull it off."

Gavin laughed loud at that one. "He be the Dread Pirate Four-Eyes."

And we were back to the pirate voice.

"That wouldn't really work," I said.

They looked at me for a moment.

"I wouldn't have four eyes," I explained. "People call people with glasses 'four-eyes' because the lenses reflect the eyes underneath. But because of the patch you couldn't see an eye, so I would only have three eyes, or maybe two eyes depending on how you count them. And the Dread Pirate Two-Eyes sounds like . . . most pirates. Well, most people. Not like anything extraordinary. You know?" I forced myself to close my mouth before I went off on how glass over your eye doesn't actually constitute another eye.

"Whatever," Travis said and pushed me. It wasn't super hard or anything, but I stumbled back a few inches.

"You're alright though, right?" Gavin asked, putting one arm around me. He used to do that when I had made a good catch and we'd walk back to the sideline. "Your eye didn't fall out or anything?"

"Kind of," I admitted, "I'm going to need surgery." Because my cornea had torn so badly, I needed a new one. It was like putting on a new windshield. Except before I could have surgery done, they had to have another cornea available. I was on some waiting list.

A replacement cornea sounded pretty awesome, but the amount of things that could go wrong had me worried. Really worried. It was like those commercials for pills where they pay the fastest-talking man in the universe to go over all of the possible ways their drug could kill you if you take it. Except this was about me and my eye, and going blind was on the list. They expected the surgery would happen in a month or so. I needed to finish my comic before then.

"Whoa. No fun," Travis said. I'm sure he wasn't actually worried about it.

"Yeah," Gavin added. "But the patch? That's crazy."

"Dread Pirate Four-Eyes," Travis repeated. I guess he didn't understand my explanation. Or he didn't care. Eventually the two broke off. "See ya later, Squint."

This was going to be a very long day.

As soon as I walked into science class, I looked for McKell. Her desk was empty. Too bad. I kind of wanted to see her, even if I'd only been a challenge.

I plopped down in my seat, pulled out my portfolio, and started working before class started.

I heard whispers about my patch.

But I had to draw. At least the best I could. Then I'd finish my comic and I'd win the contest and everyone would regret making fun of me.

I tilted my head and got to it.

Flashes of light burst through the dark as Gunn and Squint fought. Rock even got in a chomp on Gunn's leg.

"Stupid rock dog," Gunn said, turning his fireball bazooka on him.

Rock dove behind a broken octopus assassin bot just in time for a fireball to blast it into a million shards of almost nothing. "A little help?" Rock barked out to Squint. "I'm going to be pebbles soon if you don't do something."

But Squint was a step ahead of him. Streams of light shot from his daggers back at Gunn. "This is for stealing the Empress and leaving me for dead."

"Ahhh!" Gunn screamed, shooting back to block the attacks.

Suddenly a stone the size of a basketball backboard slammed into Squint, throttling him to the side. He barely stayed conscious.

He knew what had hit him. Another Centurion had shown up. Traz. A punch from the gloves of his former friend sent large stones careening toward anyone he attacked. Another stone rocketed toward Squint.

His head still swirling, Squint barely leapt to the side and his cape maneuvered under him. The boulder rushed past, close enough that he could feel the breeze from its momentum.

Awesome action. I was proud of that one.

Squint soared and dodged as his two former friends attacked, but they had capes like his. Traz joined him in the skies, while Gunn attacked from below. As Squint swooped past Gunn, he noticed something strange. Something was different about the back of his neck.

After another swoop, he got a better look. He still wasn't sure what he saw. It seemed like a group of black scales on the back of Gunn's neck.

"What's growing on your neck?" Squint asked, firing his daggers.

COMIC RULE: Even during the most intense battle

ever, comic-book characters take the time to have a conversation.

"What are you talking about?" Gunn asked. "Are you trying to distract me?"

As he soared by Traz, Squint saw that the boulder-punching Centurion had it too.

I loved the mystery of the black scales. I still had to decide when Squint was going to figure out what they were.

Rock leapt from his hiding place and raced at Gunn. He wanted to take him by surprise, but Gunn heard him and leveled his bazooka at the rock dog. This was it.

"Nooooooo!" Squint screamed and dove at Gunn, firing his light-daggers as fast as possible. He was able to knock his former friend off his feet, but got slammed by one of Traz's boulders at the same time. Squint careened from his cape and was pinned against the wall.

The right side of his face seared with pain. His vision blurred and started to fade.

He hadn't been clever enough. Not fast enough. Not good enough.

"We left you alone," Traz said, now standing over him. "You should have stayed away." Apparently, a blurry version of his former friend would be the last thing he ever saw.

I heard my teacher say something, but I was in the middle of this. Squint was trapped in a desperate situation.

> A diamond hand punched out from nowhere and Traz went flying.
>
> "I don't think this fight is fair," a female voice said. As Squint fell unconscious, he saw what he thought was a girl entirely covered in diamond. She wasn't sparkly like the gem on the end of a ring, but uncut rock naturally formed in the shape of a girl.

"Flint," an adult voice said.

"Here," I said, sketching my new character. She was hard to draw. I wasn't that good at girls, and drawing one that looked like uncut diamond wasn't easy. But I really thought she was working. I tilted my head again to try to see a bit better. I had to admit, McKell had a great idea.

"This isn't the beginning of class," Mrs. Brunner said. I looked up. Of course it wasn't. I'd been sitting in her class for at least eight minutes while she went over some announcements.

Oh.

"I'm passing back your tests," Mrs. Brunner said. "Come and get yours." She raised a stapled sheaf of paper.

I wanted to punch the desk. Completely embarrassing. Worse than back when my eyes were going bad and I hadn't even realized Gavin had thrown the ball to me in a football game. It had nearly hit me in the back—I hadn't even tried to catch it. This was worse. I was wearing an eye patch with glasses over it, and I answered my teacher like she was taking attendance when she was trying to hand me a test. I jumped up from my front corner seat and walked toward the center of the room.

Something hard slammed into my hip. I swallowed a grunt and bit my lip.

"You okay?" A girl in my class asked, but I didn't turn around.

"Watch out for those desks that jump out at ya," someone said. Neither Gavin nor Travis was in my class, but there always seemed to be someone like them or trying to be like them.

"Be respectful," Mrs. Brunner said, correcting whoever said it.

MIDDLE-SCHOOL RULE: If something terribly embarrassing can possibly happen, it will.

Apparently, I had walked into the corner of another desk. Hadn't seen that coming. It had taken me by surprise like the boulder that hit Squint. I bit the inside of my mouth, trying to hide the pain, and grabbed my test. I narrowed my eyes, trying to make out my grade in red ink at the top of the page. I didn't want to bring it right up to my face where I might be able to make it out. Not with everyone watching. Plus, I needed to make sure I noticed any desks that might attack me on the way back.

When I made it to my seat without incident, I checked the page again.

C+.

Ugh.

I used to get good grades. Of course, that was back in elementary school when I could see what the teacher wrote on the board.

"McKell Panganiban," Mrs. Brunner said. She had obviously practiced that last name before. "McKell." She held another test in her hand. "Oh," her voice dropped a little, "that's right."

What did that mean? Did the teacher know why McKell was gone? I hoped it was a family vacation, but something about the way Mrs. Brunner spoke didn't make it seem like a happy reason. I hoped McKell wasn't sick or something.

I looked back at my drawing. I was going to make the next panel completely black, like Squint's hopes and consciousness. It was deep and symbolic and stuff.

During the entire lecture, I kept glancing at McKell's empty desk—and sneaking in a little more drawing time. If I was always this distracted, I would definitely need a science tutor.

After class, I couldn't take it anymore. I walked up to Mrs. Brunner. "Hey, Mrs. Brunner, I have a question for you."

"Sure," she said. "And I meant to ask—are you okay?"

"Yeah," I said. I was grateful she didn't ask in front of the whole class. "My cornea tore. Now I'm waiting to have surgery."

"Oh. Wow." Her brows lifted. "I'm sorry. How serious is the surgery?"

"Well," I paused a second, "I hope I'll be okay. I need a new cornea, so right now I'm waiting for a donor."

Mrs. Brunner exhaled a little longer than normal. "That's pretty intense. Anything I can do?"

I shook my head, but appreciated that she asked. Students never did.

"I hope it all goes well," Mrs. Brunner said. "And keep me updated. When you have to miss some class, I can make sure you get the notes and homework."

"Thanks," I said. Then I stood there more awkwardly than I liked. "Um." How should I ask this? I opened my mouth and let the words tumble out. "How long has McKell been gone? Not that it's really my business. I'm just curious."

Mrs. Brunner looked at me for a moment before answering. "She's been gone as long as you have."

"Is she okay?" I asked.

Mrs. Brunner looked at me for a moment. I tried to read her eyes, but though my left eye had been better than my right, it still had its issues. "It's not really my place to answer that," she said. That sounded serious. Like my surgery serious. Was McKell going through something like that?

But I didn't know how to find out. I could wait until she came back to school, but I didn't want to. If she was going through something tough I wanted to know about it. "Could you give me her number so I could call her?" I asked.

Mrs. Brunner shook her head. "Sorry," she said. "I have that information, but only because I'm her teacher. I can't give it out."

"What if I ask the office?" I asked.

She shook her head again. "Same answer."

"Okay," I said.

"Hopefully she'll be back soon," Mrs. Brunner said. "But I do feel comfortable telling you that she could probably use a good friend when she comes back."

I nodded, though I wasn't really sure what that meant.

CHAPTER 12

THURSDAY

I hadn't even made it to my next class when my leg vibrated. Well, not my leg. My pocket. A text.

It was probably my mom. Grandma and Grandpa had called and told her about my torn cornea and she'd said she would come by and visit. She hadn't. No surprise there. She *had* texted me to say she was sorry it had happened. And she sent me a picture of herself with some new boyfriend in front of a random piece of street art. I guess she was trying to cheer me up.

I hadn't texted back.

I didn't know if I wanted to see whatever random thing she texted now.

I waited until I got into class and pulled out my phone. I didn't want to try to squint and walk at the same time.

It wasn't from Mom.

It was from Grandma. That was different. She never texted during school. And unlike everyone else in the world, she always took the time to write out every word. No shortcuts. All caps. I think her phone has been stuck that way since she first tried to use caps. And she punctuated everything.

> WE'VE GOT NEWS.
> WE'VE GOT A CORNEA
> AND YOU'RE SCHEDULED
> FOR SURGERY ON
> THURSDAY. IT MAKES ME
> NERVOUS, BUT WE'VE GOT
> TO DO IT.

I looked at my phone in disbelief. It was going to happen, and much sooner than anyone had thought. Just a few days away. A mix of excitement and terror filled me. I looked down at my portfolio case resting against my desk. I wasn't done with my comic. Not even close. Squint was in more trouble than ever.

I looked back down at one word on my phone—
THURSDAY.

If all went well, I could be back in this school sooner than later, seeing and drawing better than ever. Hopefully that would still be enough time to finish Squint's story before the competition deadline.

Or maybe I would never see out of my right eye again.

Cue the fast-talking commercial guy telling me everything that could go wrong.

CHAPTER 13

KERATOPLASTY

Grandma's knees bounced as we waited in brightly colored chairs in one of the examining rooms.

"When you've been injured," Grandpa said, "sometimes surgery needs to happen and then you can come back better than ever. For example, when Drew Brees hurt his shoulder, a lot of people thought he was done. But he recovered and he went on to lead the Saints to the Super Bowl and won offensive player of the year. And then there's Peyton Manning and Tom Brady who . . ."

"That's enough," Grandma said. "Unless one of them took a football to the eye, I don't want to hear it." She was breathing faster than I was and she wasn't even going under the knife . . . err, laser.

But it didn't stop Grandpa. He told at least two more stories of players recovering from injuries. And he mentioned how his friend growing up recovered from a broken collarbone. And that one had nothing to do with football. Maybe he was nervous too.

But I knew Grandpa wasn't telling the other true stories. The stories where an injury ended a player's whole career or a friend didn't recover. I'd heard those too.

"Is Mom coming?" I asked. I didn't really expect her, but I asked anyway.

"She said she would," Grandma said. "But she might be running late."

"Or she's out at some party and she'll never show," Grandpa said.

Grandma glared at Grandpa. "At one o'clock in the afternoon?" She brought her hands to her chest then wiped them on her skirt. "Goodness, I'm so sweaty, my palms are slicker than a greased waterslide."

Her jittering wasn't helping. I was the one about to have his eye cut open. I held my not-sweaty hands firmly in my lap and prayed that everything would be okay.

Soon enough I was on a table and Doctor Something—I couldn't remember his name—leaned over me, looking into some huge microscope over my eye.

"Aren't I supposed to be asleep or something?" I asked. Maybe I *was* just as nervous as Grandma. Probably. But I think that's understandable. They were going to cut out part of my eye and replace it. And who knew if it would work?

"We'll do that soon," Doctor Something said. "But you shouldn't be able to feel anything by now. Watch this." He shifted and moved over my eye. "Did you feel that?"

"What?" I asked.

"Exactly," he said. "I just touched your eye, but you couldn't feel it." The numbing drops he'd put in a few minutes before had done their job. Which was good. Very good. I did not want to feel this. And the throbbing headache that had grown worse and worse since my cornea tore had calmed down. Let's hear it for numbing drops.

I had watched a bunch of this kind of surgery online. Mostly when I should have been working on my comic. It's called a keratoplasty. That's the technical name for it, anyway. And I was really glad Grandma hadn't watched any of them with me.

All of my body would be pretty much covered up in hospital surgery blanket things except for my one eye. That would look creepy. Just a sheet with an eye staring out—seemed like a good visual I could use for a comic sometime.

The doctor would use little pads and clamps to keep my right eye open throughout the surgery. It reminded me of a mad scientist doing experiments. Again, I was glad for those numbing drops. The pads and clamps would also keep me from moving my eye during the surgery even though I was asleep. If it moved, that would be very, very bad.

"I'm going to put your mask on now," one of the doctors announced. She put a mask over my nose and mouth. "Just breathe normally."

I never thought about how I breathed until someone told me to do it normally. It was hard since I knew what was going to happen next.

It was just plain eerie to think of the surgeon fiddling with my eye. Even eerier with all of his assistants around. The doctor would rest a metal ring on top of my eye for extra security. Of course he could have put it on already and I wouldn't know. I couldn't feel it.

The doctor's assistants shifted a large white machine on a metal stand until it was over me. It had a lens in the bottom and a screen on the side for the doctor to use. Was this the laser? I'd always wanted to be able to play with lasers. It was kind of like Squint and his light-daggers. Thankfully these would be much smaller and a lot more controlled. Of course, I never wanted to be the thing the lasers played on. But I had read that professionals could program them to be far more accurate than any doctor's steady hand. And I really wanted this to be as accurate as possible. The laser would make a very careful circle at just the right depth and just the right diameter to remove my cornea.

My eyes felt heavy. Maybe the sleeping gas was working.

Part of me was furious that I was here. I hadn't finished my comic. I didn't have enough time. And the deadline was coming up and who knew what would happen.

But I couldn't change that now.

Then it would be time for the new cornea, the new windshield. Well, at least new to me. Back when the doctor told me I would need a cornea transplant I had asked him where they would get it. He said, "Walmart." Yeah, right. I'm sure he's used that joke over and over. I couldn't imagine how that would work. *Sure, you go down aisle thirteen, look to the right, and pick out your new cornea. They're right next to the metal lungs and just before the tooth crowns.* "We find a donor," the doctor eventually corrected.

"Who is going to donate the front of their eye?" I asked. I couldn't imagine anyone doing that. "Wouldn't they kind of need it?"

"Well," the doctor said. "They decide to be a donor when they're alive, but we don't use it until after they've passed away. And we can use the corneas from most people. It doesn't have to be a boy, or even a young person. You could get a cornea from a sixty-year-old woman, or a teenage girl. As long as that cornea is healthy, we can use it."

I'd been trying not to think about the dead person part. Especially since I was going to have a part of a dead person on my eye. That would make me part zombie, right? Zombie boy. Maybe I would be able to see into the worlds of the undead afterward. Another good idea for a comic.

Then the creepiest part of the surgery—eye stitches. Seriously, eye stitches. That was the hardest part for me to watch online. I shuddered just thinking about it.

After they were done, there would be a long list of stuff I couldn't do. Even bending over could change the pressure in my eye and lead to a bunch of bad complications. And of course I'd have to come back the next day for my follow-up appointment to see how well it had all worked.

Another yawn. I was falling asleep for sure.

I just hoped the last thing I'd ever see out of my right eye wasn't the ceiling of the operating room.

CHAPTER 14

UNWRAPPED

My eye was so wrapped up I had no idea if I was blind or not. So as we drove back to the eye center for my day-after-surgery follow-up in the old Nissan Sentra, I tried to distract myself. I wondered how Squint would feel after he met the person who saved him. I imagined it over and over. He would wake up and find a girl who looked like uncut diamond.

"You owe me one," the diamond girl said, her nearly transparent lips moving with every word.

As Squint got a good look at her, he thought he could see her light brown face and white suit beneath the diamond.

Squint shook his head, trying to focus his foggy

mind. "What happened? Who are you?" He lay in some high-tech infirmary with a hydration blanket over the top of him giving off healing steam. His hair all tousled and bandages on the side of his head, he sat up with a lot of effort.

"I'm Diamond," she said, and offered him a diamond handshake. Who shook hands anymore? But he shook it. "And I managed to get you and your rock dog out of there before those two crazies killed you." She smiled. "You're welcome."

"Thank you," Squint said, grabbing his head to try to keep it from ringing.

"It was foolish of you to go in there alone," Diamond said.

Squint shook his head. "I didn't go in there alone. I went with Rock."

"You know what I mean," Diamond said.

"Hey, wait," Squint added. "Didn't *you* go in alone?"

"That's beside the point. I'm invincible." She tapped her hard exterior.

Her diamond casing was impressive. "How did you get your powers?" Squint asked.

Diamond shook her head. "Let's not pry. We just met each other."

"But—" Squint started.

"And there's something you should see," Diamond said and handed him a mirror. Squint looked at the bandages covering half of his face, but especially over his eye.

"I'm trained in magical surgery," Diamond said. "I did what I could, but unfortunately, your eye will never be the same."

I thought that maybe I should give Squint more powers after the surgery. Maybe he could see the future through his new eye. Or he could see past walls. Or even see through other people's eyes.

I'd have to decide. Of course I'd have a lot of time to think about it, while my eye was healing. If it was going to heal.

As we were walking into the doctor's office, I got another text. From my mom.

> Hey Flinty, I'm sooooo
> sorry I missed ur surgery. 😞
> But G-ma said it went great.
> I'll come by later with a gift.
> ♡ u!

She gave me no reason why she'd missed it. And no apology. And I doubted she'd come by with a gift. Not that she never brings me gifts—it's that she promises a lot of things she never does.

When we sat down in the waiting room, I erased the text. I didn't want to reread it later and get upset.

Eventually, a gray-haired lady led my grandparents and me into a treatment room. Fifteen minutes later, some of the doctor's assistants got to work pulling the tape off from around my eye. It felt like a radioactive octopus sucker being ripped, one tentacle at a time, from the swollen area around my eye. Sensitive stuff. I think I lost half of my eyebrow, but my right eye wasn't covered anymore.

My pulse raced as I slowly started to open my right eye. This was the moment of truth. I half expected to be blind. Or now was the time I got supernatural eye powers. I felt like Squint when the Empress first gave him his light-daggers. Or when she gave him Rock.

The light hit me hard. It was painful, but . . . BAZAAM! I could see! I blinked over and over. Now I hoped I could see well.

My eye went in and out of focus, but that was probably because it had been covered so long. It felt goopy as the doctor inspected his handiwork. "That's looking really good, Flint. Can you see okay?" I nodded. I had to blink away a few blurs. There was something about his smile that seemed happier than I expected. Maybe he really was excited for how well it turned out.

"How does it feel?" Grandma asked.

"Fine," I said. Which was only partially true. I had more of a dull pain than before, and something was dripping from my eye.

"He told me this morning that it hurt," Grandma said, making me sound like a liar. Did she always have that many wrinkles around her eyes? Maybe this surgery stuff had aged her.

"That's actually to be expected," the doctor said, still looking me over. He wiped up the goop coming from my eye with a tissue.

"Good to hear," Grandpa said. His face was wrinkly too. And I hadn't noticed how many little wisps of hair he had coming out of his ears. He looked much older today for some reason. Older—and there was something about his eyes.

My breath caught in my throat. They weren't older. The doctor wasn't happier. I could see better. So much better.

Three things happened so quickly I couldn't tell you which came first. My lips curled into a smile, a huge one. My chest felt like it filled with a tingly helium, growing and lifting. And my nose started to run. The last one might have had to do with my weepy eye, but maybe not.

"These drops are to prevent infection," the doctor said, moving to write stuff on a pad of paper. "Your body is dealing with something new and we need to help it."

He kept talking, but I wasn't listening. I was looking at nearly everything in the room. The surgery only happened yesterday and already I could see so much better. My hands had pores. The carpet had intertwining circles and dots, not "vomit-speckled" like I'd described it to Grandma on an earlier visit. The wall was textured. The wood desk had dark grain marks in it. I had completely forgotten that furniture had those. It was like my life had started all over again.

A chuckle. "Has your vision improved?" the doctor asked.

I nodded.

He laughed again. "By the way you're looking around, I think it's improved quite a bit. We don't always know right away."

It had been *years* since I had seen this clearly. I closed my right eye to see the difference between it and my left. My left eye was still fuzzy, especially without my glasses on, and my vision went a little double. It wasn't nearly as bad as my right had been. But when I opened my right eye again, it dominated. I could see so much better.

I looked over at Grandpa and Grandma. Was she crying? "This is a downright bless-the-heavens miracle," she said.

Grandpa hugged her from the side. "Just like Drew Brees," he mumbled to himself.

"Should we test this vision out?" the doctor asked.

I nodded, grinning like an idiot. I hadn't actually ever wanted an eye test before. In elementary school, when I had to take them, I used to try to memorize what the kid in front of me said and repeat it. I couldn't read enough on my own. But this one felt different. I could actually do this.

The doctor stood and turned the electric eye chart on. "Flint, it's good to see you so happy."

He had no idea.

After doing better on the eye test than I'd done in a very, very long time, I looked past everyone to see the separate tiles on the ceiling. Ouch! Lights. Too bright.

"You'll still be quite sensitive to light," the doctor said, noticing what had just happened. He reached across his computer and grabbed a pair of sunglasses. They reminded me of the safety glasses we use in woodshop, but tinted. "You'll need these for the next few weeks. They'll protect you from dust, light, anything hitting your eye." He found another patch. "And sleep with this patch taped on so you don't hurt anything in your sleep." He handed the patch to Grandma.

I held the glasses in my hand. I wasn't ready to dim my vision just yet.

"But what about his regular glasses?" Grandma asked.

"His right eye is great now, but it will take a little while until we know how much his prescription has changed," the doctor said. "The eye has to settle a little. I'm hopeful that he may not need correction at all in that eye. It may get even better than it is now. If he feels like he can see well enough, he can wear the sunglasses I gave him, and put his contact in his left eye."

"He doesn't like wearing his contacts," Grandma said.

"I'm fine," I said. She was right, but I didn't need her worried about me.

"Or if that's too irritating, we can punch the right lens out of his glasses," the doctor said, "and he could wear the sunglasses over them."

I nodded. That sounded weird, but we could worry about that later.

The doctor kept talking. "Also—you can't bend over for at least a few weeks. Don't pick anything up off the ground, don't tie your shoes, don't try to lift anything." This was repeated instruction from before. "It will change the pressure in your eye. Oh, and especially—no lifting weights."

For some reason, Grandpa thought that last one was really

funny. "Flint doesn't lift weights," he said. Thankfully the doctor kept going.

"Take it easy. No strenuous running or exercise. And you'll want to adjust your wardrobe as well for the next little while. Button-up shirts so you don't have to pull anything over your head. Elastic-waist pants so that you can remove them easily without bending over. Slip-on shoes so your laces don't get untied."

Whoa, that list was intense. And dorky. Grandma's brow furrowed. I doubted we had the money for a new wardrobe as well as a new eye. I don't think she was worried about the dorky part.

The doctor wheeled over on his rolling stool close to me again and looked at my eye. I noticed the embroidery on his white coat.

Dr. John Young, M.D.
Corneal Surgeon

Now I might be able to remember his name. We got some last instructions and hit the road. Despite wearing the sunglasses, I kept my eyes closed most of the way home. The light outside was harsher than inside the dim doctor's office, but I did peek once in a while. I couldn't help myself. I wanted to see the leaves on the trees, the layers in the clouds, and the gravel off the side of the road. I wanted to see the clean lines of the store signs, the fabric weave of my shirt sleeves, the way light bounced off of all of the little bumps on the fake leather of the dashboard. I kept stealing glances at my grandma's and grandpa's faces. Still older and more tired than I thought. But also more—I could see so much more of them.

Tears gathered in the corner of my eyes. Not because they were dry and irritated but because I was so happy. I would have given the Hulk a bath just to look at the suds on his brown fur. I *hated* giving the Hulk his bath, but I was *that* happy.

The doctor had said my eye might get even better.

Better. That just felt unreal.

An idea flicked through my mind, something else I wanted to see. I was immediately antsy.

"When we get home," Grandma said, "you should write a letter to the family of whoever gave you that cornea."

"Absolutely," I said. I was so grateful I would have done an interpretational thank-you dance for them if that was what they wanted. But then reality hit. "Wait—we don't know who they are." Grandma had already asked the doctor about the donor and was told there were laws that kept everything anonymous.

"True," Grandma said, "but we can write a letter and the doctor's staff can deliver it for us. If the family decides that it's okay then we might even be able to meet them one day."

"Like Deion Branch," Grandpa said, "saying thank you."

"Okay," I said.

We pulled into the carport and I jumped out of the car and ran into the house. There was something in my room I had to see. And this time I wouldn't have to squint.

CHAPTER 15

OFF

The Hulk barked at me and I could see him better than ever. That crazy gamma-ray bulldog almost looked like he was smiling at me. Or drooling at me. Or both.

I said hello super-fast, rubbed his chubby bulldog cheeks, then ran down the hall. His bath would have to wait. Maybe for a long time. Nobody had asked me to do it, anyway. "Don't run!" Grandma yelled after me. "You heard what the doctor said! Don't run. Don't run."

She could call out all she wanted to. I had somewhere to . . . I slowed when I was only a few steps from my room. I had to push against the wall to keep myself steady. My head pounded. Apparently, there was a good reason for the no-running advice, especially a day after surgery—my body wasn't ready for that.

After a minute, I seemed to be alright. I walked into my room slowly and stared at my desk. My comic pages were sitting right in the center in neat stacks. I wouldn't have to squint to see them. I wouldn't have to tilt or twist. I wouldn't have to focus through double vision.

Technically, I wasn't supposed to read or write for a while. It would strain my eye too much. But the doctor didn't say anything about drawing. He especially didn't say anything about *looking* at drawings. My heart was pounding.

I sat down and closed my eyes for a moment, getting ready to get a good look at my work. I imagined Squint and the countless hours I'd spent drawing the underappreciated hero. I thought about all he had been through. And how much more time it was going to take to finish his story and be able to show it to the world. It was worth it. All this double vision, all the doctor visits—even the surgery had been worth it.

I opened wide and picked up the first sheet on the top. It was my latest sketch. Squint had just been saved by a diamond arm.

The layout was great. There was action and depth. But something was off.

My right eye was blurry with moisture so I blinked a few times, then used the back of my hand to wipe it away gently.

Better.

I looked at the page again. My heart slowed. I twisted the

page and looked at it from different angles. I took off the protective glasses.

Squint was off. Disproportionate. Some of the angles and lines weren't right at all. And that wasn't the end. The whole page was off. Lines weren't sharp. This wasn't what I drew. It couldn't be.

Maybe it was only the last few pages as my eyes deteriorated. I grabbed the next page on the stack. The metal castle was slightly tilted. It didn't loom or look foreboding when it leaned—it looked like it was about to tip over. It's tough for a hero to look awesome when the bad guy might be defeated by his own faulty architecture.

Squint's shoulders weren't square. He looked almost like a slight hunchback.

Awful.

I grabbed another page.

Awful.

Another.

Awful.

Another.

Awful.

Wrong angles, smudgy shading, lines didn't match up.

I thought I was good. I'd been so delusional. A real comic-book artist could have drawn these with his toes. Blindfolded. And they probably would have looked better. My drawings seemed like a third grader had scribbled them out.

My eyes stung, both of them. How come nobody told me? McKell didn't tell me. Grandma and Grandpa didn't tell me.

I crumpled the paper in my hand. That felt good. I crushed it hard, my fingers turning red with the pressure.

I grabbed the stacks and flung them to the ground.

So much work. So, so much work. So many hours. So much heart. I slammed my hands down hard on my desk.

I had a new Comic Rule.

COMIC RULE: Actually know how to draw.

"What's with all the drama in here?" Grandma asked, opening the door. Everything boiled up inside me. I could finally see. And what I wanted to see most wasn't worth looking at.

"You lied to me," I said. And she had. She had been the first one to tell me that I was good at drawing.

CHAPTER 16

AN ALMOST SUPERPOWER

What is the first phase of mitosis?

a) Anaphase

b) Interphase

c) Prophase

d) Telophase

e) I-don't-care-at-all-phase

Okay, so that last one wasn't on the worksheet, but if it was I would have circled it. We had a substitute in science and the hour was filled with silent worksheets. Painfully boring. Add that to the fact that I still had to wear the safety sunglasses, even indoors, because the light bothered me and we couldn't risk anything getting in my eye. Underneath those I had on my old glasses with the right lens missing. And I was wearing my grandma's flannel shirt (that I hoped no one could tell was a girl's shirt) with a new pair of slip-on canvas shoes and elastic waistband jeans that my grandma bought for me so I wouldn't have to bend over. I'm sure I was looking pretty hot. What a way to come back to school.

McKell was back too. I looked over at her. She was even prettier than the fuzzy version of her I could see before. She wore a blue-and-white striped shirt with a white hair tie holding up her dark hair. For a second, I could see something else. Her thick lashes were close together as her eyes seemed heavy and her dark eyebrows rested low. She moved slowly when she tucked a loose strand of hair behind her ear.

Was she okay? Maybe I could check on her after class, but I didn't think she would want me to talk to her where everyone could see.

Was this seeing thing kind of like a superpower? I could see wrinkles, and smiles, and sleepy eyes. It almost made it so I could see how people felt. Or at least it gave me more clues. It was definitely more than I was used to.

McKell looked up. I gave a sly wave. Hopefully it wasn't too obvious, just in case she was still trying to keep everything on the down low.

She looked at me a moment, probably surprised by my weird sunglasses, or my outfit, or both. Then she did a quick check to see if anyone was watching and waved back. But there was something off about it. Her smile was tiny—no teeth. Maybe she was feeling sick or something.

The sub finished up as the bell rang.

I took longer than I really needed to gather my stuff so I could leave at the same time McKell did. Maybe I shouldn't have. I mean, I did look like a total weirdo. But I hadn't seen her in a really long time.

She was so slow; we were pretty much the last ones walking out of the room.

"Hey," I said, nodding and smiling.

"Hey," she said. She tried to grin, but didn't get very far.

I knew that I didn't have much time to talk with her before we stepped out into the hall and she wouldn't want to be seen with me. "I haven't seen you in a while," I said.

"Have you seen much?" she asked, pointing at my glasses. Her voice sounded a little flatter than normal.

"I got surgery on my eye," I said, pointing at it. "I can see a *lot* better now."

"Really? That's cool," she said. "I figured that there was some crazy reason that you were wearing sunglasses in class." She tapped the side of her head. "I mean, it's quite the fashion statement."

I nodded. "You look great," I said, then almost immediately regretted it. "I mean, I'm not trying to say anything awkward. I'm just saying that I can see you better than before and you look good." Terrible. Anything I could say next wouldn't help. "Oh, my gosh. It's not like that. I mean . . . that it's good to see you. And I like your shirt." *I like your shirt?* "And your hair." Oh, that fixes everything. I closed my mouth before I would say anything else.

"Thanks," she said. A hint of this smile was real.

We were leaving the classroom and I didn't quite know what to do next. Did she want me to pretend not to know her? Did we split up here?

We walked through the door and she didn't seem to mind.

KAPOW! Oh, yeah! I was wearing crazy sunglasses and my grandma's shirt and McKell was okay walking with me. We were definitely friends. At least a little bit. I wasn't just a challenge, right? "So what about you?" I asked. "Why were you gone for so long?"

Almost immediately she wiped her eyes.

Oh, no. Wrong thing to ask. "I'm sorry," I said. "I didn't want to make you upset. I just don't know. I haven't seen you since the hike."

"It's not your fault," she said. She sniffled again and turned to the wall. She wasn't walking anymore.

"Do you want me to help you with another challenge?" I asked. I was still kind of surprised that we were talking in public.

She shook her head. "I'm not doing those anymore."

"What?" I asked. "Why not?" I had been online a few times looking at some of Danny's other videos. I didn't see any new ones, but there were plenty of old ones to do. It helped me pass the time while I was recovering, especially since I didn't want to draw. "Maybe we could try the one—"

"Danny died," she said, interrupting me.

I froze.

Once in a football game, I got knocked to the ground so hard I couldn't breathe. It was like all my air rushed out of me. Suddenly I felt like that.

I wanted to pause time, let the world slow, let my heart sag, feel heavy.

The cheerful conversations around us seemed out of place.

"He wasn't doing well," she said. "So I took a few days off of school to be with him. And then," she sniffled, "he left." She started walking again.

I could only imagine what it must feel like to be McKell right now. No wonder she seemed different.

What do you say to someone after their brother dies? Maybe if I had some time and I was writing a comic about it I could come up with something perfect, the best thing to say. But in the moment, I had no idea. I wanted to go tell my grandma because she always made pies for people who were going through hard things. If I had a pie, maybe it would have been easier. "I'm sorry," was all that came out.

"McKell, what are you doing with Squint?" Gavin asked, coming up beside us. "I mean, Mr. Sunglasses McCool."

This timing couldn't have possibly been worse. And Travis was with him. I tried to think quickly. I could tell them that McKell was tutoring me again, but in the hallway? Would they go for that? But McKell didn't need teasing. Not now.

"We're walking," she said before I could say anything. She didn't even seem worried or embarrassed. Just emotionless.

"You still tutoring the pirate?" Travis asked. Good. He remembered about the tutoring thing. Maybe that would help. "Well, he used to be a pirate. Now Squint's Mr. Shades. I don't think he can decide what he is."

Anger bubbled inside me. They had no class. If they thought something was funny they just said it, no matter how much damage they caused. "Leave us alone," I said. I never said stuff like that, but it just came out.

"Us?" Gavin asked and he raised his eyebrows. "McKell, is there something you need to tell us?"

I had been teased by these guys for years and I could take it pretty well, but when they were teasing McKell right after I found out her brother died, something inside of me burst.

"Lay off!" I said. "It's not like that."

They stopped for a second and looked. "Whoa," Travis said, "Squint's getting mean."

Some of the people passing slowed and watched us.

Gavin and Travis had to know that Danny had died. They were McKell's friends.

"Get out of here," I said.

"Calm down," Gavin said.

"Just leave," I said, pointing down the hall.

"You can't command me, Cap'n," Travis said using his pirate voice. "You're not wearing your patch."

"It's alright," McKell said to me and them. She was too calm, not herself.

"Nah," Gavin said. "We're out."

And they left.

McKell walked up to her locker, not seeming bothered by the whole thing. Which was good, I guess. I glanced down the hall at the backs of Gavin and Travis.

"Don't they know?" I asked McKell.

"Yeah," she said. "They know. They're just dorks sometimes." She put her books in the locker. "And you didn't make things better by yelling at them."

Did I do something wrong?

"I've got to go," she said. "See ya later, Squint."

And she left too.

She didn't seem mad at me, but I still had no idea if we were actually friends.

Did it matter? It wasn't like we would talk much anymore. She wasn't doing any more challenges and I didn't want to draw.

CHAPTER 17

FROM THE DEAD

I leaned back on the pillows on my bed, throwing a football up and catching it. It had been on my bookshelf for a long time. My depth perception was a little tricky with only the one good eye, but I was so much better at catching now. Still, if Grandma saw me throwing a ball above my new eye she'd kill me. Maybe now that my double vision was gone in my right eye, I could throw the ball around on the field; play a few games. Well, when I healed. I kind of doubted it though, considering the safety warden I lived with. She'd never let me take a tackle.

My phone was reading Danny's obituary to me. I highlighted the text and it said the words. I still wasn't supposed to do much reading.

Danny Panganiban, an amazing son, brother, and friend died due to heart disease. He loved the outdoors, sports (especially watching the Nebraska Huskers!), jokes, movies, and making videos for his successful YouTube channel, "Danny's Challenges." Danny had progeria, a rare genetic disease. It is what gave Danny his unique look, and unfortunately caused his body to age much faster than it should. Though many may have clicked on Danny's channel because of his looks, they loved him for something much more.

Every week Danny would share details about his life and challenge anyone who would listen. He challenged people to be kinder, braver, and more helpful. His almost half a million subscribers came to know him, and became better people because they took his challenges.

The obituary went on to share where Danny's funeral would be (which I had already missed) and mentioned his mother, father, McKell, and grandparents.

A short knock, then Grandpa stepped into my room, almost completely filling the doorframe.

As I gripped the ball and sat up, my feet swung over the edge of my bed and landed on the comic pages that I'd left on the ground.

"Mind if I take a seat?" Grandpa asked, pointing at the other side of my bed.

"Go for it," I said.

He carefully avoided stepping on the comic pages as he made his way to my bed and sat. "I haven't seen you play with that ball in a while." He opened his hands for a toss and I lobbed it to him. "Nice lateral."

"It's been collecting dust on my bookshelf," I said.

Grandpa nodded. "Grandma said that you haven't picked up your drawings." He threw the ball up and down ignoring the papers scattered all over the floor. "She said you're upset because you don't think you're very good at it."

I didn't answer. Every time I looked at those pages it was like my blood froze and boiled at the same time.

"Well," he said, reaching down to pick up a page, "I know you can't bend over while your eye is recovering, so I thought I'd help."

"Don't bother," I said.

He looked at me for a moment then picked up another. He flattened both of them on his lap, then set them on the bed next to him. "I'm no art critic and I like your art, but I'm not going to tell you a lot of blah, blah, blah," he said. "You're talented. But whether you believe you are or not, I think you ought to keep your drawings." He picked up another paper. This time a little sigh slipped out. He did that sometimes as he bent over. "You worked hard on these. That's something you should be proud of."

"But they aren't any good—" I started.

"Hard work," he interrupted, his voice louder, "is always something you should be proud of. Now maybe they weren't exactly what you hoped for, but if you were to work hard again, maybe they would be." He picked up the rest of the pages without another word and set them on the corner of my desk. Then he left without closing the door behind him.

Kind of a strange talk.

I looked at the pages on my bed for a moment. I looked at my pencils and my pens. I *had* worked hard. What other kid with my eye problems would even try? Maybe he was right.

I picked a page up. The lines of Squint's arm didn't meet right. One of the panel's outlining boxes was tilted.

Nope.

I dropped the page.

Back to my bed and the ball.

My phone beeped.

I pulled up the screen. Inside a bubble were the words: "Watch a new post from 'Danny's Challenges.'"

I clicked it without thinking. It would be a nice distraction.

Wait. How was there a new video? Danny wasn't around anymore. My phone had read me his obituary. His family buried him. This had to be some weird glitch.

Danny's face appeared, nearly taking up the whole screen. I couldn't help it. I clicked on the arrow to make the video play.

"I bet you didn't expect to see me, did you?" Danny said, his wide smile still on his face. "I didn't think so." He wagged a popsicle-stick finger.

What was going on? How could this post even be here?

"Well," Danny continued, "if you're watching this it means that I'm not around anymore." He took in a deep breath. "I'm dead." He looked off to one side. "That sounds really weird coming out of my mouth, but I've been planning on it for a long time. I've counted on it. I planned my whole funeral, including all the songs." There was a cut to him bobbing his head while some twangy country song played. Then a clip of him rocking out to some hard metal song. Then him looking really concerned while the Munchkins from *The Wizard of Oz* sang, "Ding, dong, the witch is dead." If it had been a better day I would have laughed out loud. "I even wrote my own you-guly . . . oo-guly. Oh, I never know how to say that. Just a minute. I'll be right back." Again, he left in his mistakes. There was a jump cut, then he sat there with a huge smile on his face and said, "Eulogy! If you were there I hope it was epic." He spread his thin arms out wide. "Best funeral ever."

I had never heard that phrase spoken before. Especially not with a smile on the speaker's face.

"I hope you had a beautiful Mass and heard some great stories at the wake," Danny said. "And I hope you smiled more than you cried." He leaned forward a little. "But I do hope you cried a little. I mean, I *am* kind of awesome."

I could guarantee that McKell cried more than a little.

"But," he said, "I found out a way to post stuff after I'm gone." The camera came in close. "I know that's both cool and a little creepy." He let out an "ooohh" sound, like a ghost haunting. Well, a very high-pitched sounding ghost. "I actually hope it will be more cool than creepy." He crossed his thin fingers. "I hope."

"But I have something to say." He scooted closer to the camera. "I—" he whispered. "I hid a million dollars in a special place and only those of you who follow my clues will ever have a chance to get it." He stared solemnly into the camera.

His face cracked into a smile. "Just kidding. I've never had close to a million dollars. And if I did, you'd better believe that I'd have paid my hospital bills, taken my family on several trips to the Bahamas, and bought my sister a whole bunch of ukuleles."

How could he be making jokes? When he filmed this, he knew he was going to die. He made extra videos for his family and his followers, and they were funny? What kind of kid was this?

"No," Danny continued. "I've thought about death for a long time and I decided to do this. I've still got some more challenges in me. And," he paused for a second, "some of you might be sad." A new challenge might be the perfect thing to help McKell.

Danny wiggled his eyebrows. "I don't want anyone moping around." The video cut to a different view. "If you *are* moping around, I'm going to come back from the dead to haunt you." He acted like a ghost again before continuing. "Here's a new challenge." His eyes danced. "I think you're going to like it."

CHAPTER 18

CHALLENGE ACCEPTED

"For this project," Mrs. Brunner said, holding up a worksheet on photosynthesis, "I want you to work with a partner."

This was a perfect opportunity. "You can propose who you might work with," Mrs. Brunner continued, "but I can either approve or deny it. Once approved, you can move desks to easily work together. Both of you read the chapter and double-check one another's answers."

I took a deep breath and raised my hand. I hadn't done that in any of my classes for a very long time.

Even with my sunglasses on I could see a small look of surprise on Mrs. Brunner's face, but she raised one finger to indicate for me to wait. "Hopefully between the two of you,

you can make sure you get them all right." She looked down at me. "Flint."

Was I really going to do this? I was surprised when the words came out. "Can I work with McKell?" I asked, my hand still raised.

A few *oohs* echoed around the class, everyone assuming I liked her. I didn't really care.

"That should be fine," Mrs. Brunner said. In fact, she might have even given me a slight smile. "As long as it's okay with her." She looked over at McKell, who nodded. She didn't smile and wave or anything, but she did nod.

I knew everyone was looking at me. Part of me wanted to play it cool, but I was actually kind of proud of myself. I almost always had to take whoever was left over after everyone else was paired up with their friends. Today, maybe *I* had a friend.

Once Mrs. Brunner let us move around, I went and sat next to McKell.

"You saw it, didn't you?" she said, her eyes wide.

It took me a second. "His post?" I nodded enthusiastically. "How did he do that?"

"I don't know," she said. "Crazy, huh?" She seemed a little better today. Maybe a little happier. Maybe it was good for her to see her brother again. She held up the assignment paper. "Let's do this."

"Before we start, I have a question for you," I said, "Do you want to watch a comedy with me? You can pick it. I don't even care which one it is. I just think you should . . . I mean, I want to . . . you know—"

She cut me off. "No." She looked at the worksheet like it was a final exam and she had better get all of the answers right.

Maybe she wasn't doing better.

The comedy was Danny's challenge. He wanted his followers to gather up with their friends and watch something funny. To talk and laugh. And if we talked about him, his rule was that we'd have to tell the fun stories. No crying allowed. It was supposed to be a night of remembering the happy, the good memories. He even listed a few of his favorite comedies as suggestions. I thought that might be nice for McKell.

"C'mon," I said. I had some leftover money from my birthday and could get us both into the second-run theater. I might even have enough left over for popcorn.

"No," McKell said. "I just don't . . ."

I thought she might not want to. She did say that she wasn't doing the challenges anymore. I reached into my portfolio, pulled out a piece of paper and slapped it on her desk, cutting her off. I almost couldn't believe I did it. I mean, it was my plan, but I actually did it.

She looked at it and back to me. I took my sunglasses off so I could see her better.

"What's this?" she asked. "Your comic?"

"And it's terrible," I said.

"It's not terrible—" she started.

"Yes, it is," I said. "I thought I was almost as good as a real comic-book artist, but everything is off. Now that I can really see, I—" I stopped talking. I swallowed to stop that weird thing that starts coming up my throat when I tear up. Nobody was supposed to cry in science. Unless we're dissecting frogs. And today we weren't dissecting frogs.

"I'm sorry," she said, "but you're being too hard on yourself. It really is good."

"Not good enough," I said. "I can't win any contest with this."

She looked at my comic and back at me. "You don't know that. You might as well—"

"That's not the point," I said. "Even if I don't like them, do you remember our deal?"

McKell got really quiet and looked at me. There was a serious argument going on behind her eyes.

"How about I finish my comic if you finish Danny's challenges?" She raised her hand to interrupt me, but I kept talking. I learned that from Grandpa. "And I know you've got the harder end, but after all my surgery and recovery and stuff, I've only got a week. I'm going to have to draw like crazy. Stay up late, the whole works. But I'll do my part if you'll do yours."

She looked at me.

"And I'll help you with your challenges," I added.

She started to shake her head again.

I reached into my portfolio case and took out another picture. I'd stayed up late getting it done. McKell stared at it for several seconds.

I had drawn a girl in a punching stance completely covered in diamond. Each muscle looked like it was part of an impenetrable stone. "She's invincible," I said. McKell kept staring. "And I need your help."

She looked up at me, then back down at my drawing.

"Please," I said.

Her chest rose and fell with a deep breath then she started to nod. "Okay, but we'll switch it," she said.

I raised one eyebrow. "You're going to start drawing comics?"

"No." She smiled a little. Microscopic but it was there. "My parents already are planning on watching a comedy with all of Danny's friends at our house tomorrow night. It's their way of doing his challenge. But I told them I wasn't going to. I planned to stay in my room. I'll tell them yes, if you'll come over," she said.

"Definitely," I said, gathering up my comic sheets before anyone else could see them.

She took another deep breath. "Deal," she said.

CHAPTER 19

COMEDY

"Here it is," Grandpa said, pulling up to a rather new two-story house. It had a gate, a fountain, and a few trees with bushes surrounding them. Every light in the house was on and cars filled the driveway and were parked along the road. Grandpa pulled in behind the cars in the driveway.

"Do you see 1367 written on the house?" Grandma asked, checking the address again.

"No, but this is it," Grandpa said. He was right. I saw the numbers. The houses in her neighborhood looked like millionaires lived there. McKell lived in a different world than I did.

"What if you get one of your headaches?" Grandma asked. "Or if your eyes start hurting?"

"He has his phone, right?" Grandpa asked.

I leaned forward from the back seat and showed her my phone. "I'll be fine. McKell's parents are here. We're watching a movie and hanging out. There really isn't anything to worry about."

Grandma stared at the house out the window. "You'll wear your glasses, right?"

"Yep." I would wear my eyeglasses with only one lens, but I had every intention of taking off my stupid sunglasses when I got in the house. Who wore sunglasses inside, at night, watching a movie? Besides, the doctor had said to wear the sunglasses for two weeks and the two weeks were over. I still had light sensitivity outside in the sun or sometimes under fluorescent lights, like at the grocery store, but most of the time I was okay without them.

Grandpa turned and spoke over his shoulder, "You better get out before your grandma locks the doors."

"Oh, stop it," Grandma said, hitting Grandpa's arm playfully with the back of her hand.

I jumped out.

"Be safe," Grandma shouted out the window. "I love you."

"He'll be fine," Grandpa said.

I turned to the house. I could hear hip-hop music beating and people talking as I made my way from the dark sidewalk to the glowing front porch. The crowd was a little intimidating, but I rang the doorbell anyway. The door opened and noise, light, and warmth hit me all at once. McKell stood there, her hair down around her face. She looked more relaxed than I had ever seen her at school.

"Come in," she said. "It's almost time for the movie." She grabbed my forearm and pulled me inside the house. I'm not sure, but I thought it was an I'm-happy-to-see-you pull in, and not a I'm-embarrassed-to-be-seen-with-you pull in. That was good. We'd talked a couple of times after science, but she still ate lunch with Gavin, Travis, Emma, and Chloe. I didn't know why. Maybe habit. I mean, they teased her like they teased everyone. As McKell closed the front door, I heard the old Nissan drive away. I took off my sunglasses and shoved them in a pocket.

"Sorry, you'll have to take off your shoes," McKell said. "House rules." She pointed to a shelf that had orderly rows of shoes stacked on every available surface and a huge pile of shoes on the floor next to it.

I sat down, careful not to do any damage to the pressure in my eye and slipped off my shoes. "There are a lot of people here," I said, pointing at all the other shoes.

"Yeah," she said. "My brother made a lot of friends. A bunch of them came out from Grand Island where we used to live." The house was well decorated. I looked up at a large wooden fork and spoon on the wall. The idea of someone eating with them made me smile.

"Isn't Grand Island like an hour away?" I asked, putting my shoes on the edge of the pile, hoping I could find them again. I'd heard of the city, but never been there. I did know it was definitely not an actual island.

"Yeah," she said, leading the way down the hall. "An hour and a half, actually."

Wow. People came from an hour and a half away to watch a movie because of Danny. Impressive. There is no way my grandparents would use that kind of gas money and that much time driving unless it was super special.

This must be super special.

"I almost thought you weren't going to make it," McKell said. The hall opened up to a great room. There were people in the kitchen, at the table, sitting on the counter, a group of girls sitting cross-legged on the floor, chatting. On the other side was a large living space. People sat on all parts of the couches and chairs, a group of what looked like cousins and aunts and uncles were singing karaoke in a corner, and teenagers were downing plates of food around the coffee table. Even more people came from a back hallway I assumed led to bedrooms or a bathroom. There were old people and a few small kids, but mostly teens. If I were to guess, there must have been more than fifty people.

McKell led me to the kitchen island that was covered in dishes of food. Cooked veggies, meat in red sauce, fried chicken or something, spaghetti with sliced hot dogs, pasta salad, and a huge dish of rice. "Eat up," she said. "Most of these people have already finished and we still have enough food to feed the whole school."

"I ate before I came," I explained. It smelled really good, even though some of it looked a little different than what I'm used to.

"I'm sorry," McKell said. "I should have told you that we would have food. We'll have to send some home with you, then. We're going to have way too much left over. If you ever come over again for a party, come hungry. We'll always have lots of food."

A boy who looked a couple of years older than us made his way over to McKell and gave her a big hug. "Man, it's good to see you, Mickey." The hug lasted a while, so I studied the small egg rolls on the plate like I was very interested in them.

Mickey? Oh. McKell, Mickey. I guess it worked.

"Good to see you too," McKell said. She pulled away, but he kept his arm across her shoulder and she kept an arm around his waist. "Squint, this is Yellow," she introduced me. I had never met this guy, but I'd heard that name before.

Yellow offered his free hand. "Your name is as strange as mine." He had fluffy black hair and a long nose. "Yellow is my last name."

I shook his hand. "Squint's just a nickname," I said. "Bad eyes." I gestured toward my one-lensed glasses. "You edited Danny's videos," I said.

"We have a subscriber to the channel here," Yellow said, pointing down at me while pretending to be making an announcement to everyone else in the house.

I nodded. "They look good. Nice work."

McKell smiled really big. "Squint doesn't really talk to people, let alone compliment them. You should feel honored."

What? That wasn't true.

Was it?

"But he is a really good comic-book artist," McKell added. She set me up for a fist bump.

I bumped my fist into hers, realizing that this was the first time anyone had ever introduced me as a great artist. It felt . . . I don't know. I didn't agree with her. My comics still needed a lot of work, but it felt nice to hear the compliment.

I noticed a small table that was set up against the wall with a picture of Danny, thick white candles flickering on both sides, and a Cornhuskers ball cap resting in front. It was the same hat that Danny wore in his videos. Nobody in my family had ever died, at least no one that I'd known, but I wondered if this table was something that only McKell's family did or if my grandparents would do it for a loved one as well.

"Thank you, everyone, for coming," a loud deep voice boomed from the kitchen. Everyone hushed and I turned around to find a tall, dark-skinned man with a hipster beard, trendy glasses, and tailor-made clothes. I bet it was McKell's dad. "Danny was always full of surprises, but this is the winner. I don't know how he posted that last challenge, but I'm glad he did. It is great to see you all somewhere other than his funeral." He got choked up a little but didn't stop. "None of that," he corrected himself. "Danny's rules."

Some people chuckled.

"Thank you," McKell's dad continued, "for being great friends and family to our boy." He cleared his throat. "The movie choice for tonight is a classic. *The Princess Bride.* Danny loved it, even if his mother didn't."

The crowd chuckled again.

"Still don't!" McKell's mom said from behind us. Everyone laughed a little harder. She was tall and slender like McKell but had pale skin, lighter than mine, and her brown hair almost had some red in it. I could see how McKell got some features from both of her parents.

I'd seen the movie before. It was pretty good. I mean, it wasn't one of the Captain Americas, or Avengers, or one of the Thors, but it was still good.

"I'm going to warm up the projector. We still have plenty of food. If you want movie treats, there are pretzels and soda for everyone. Danny was allergic to corn, so we're more of a soft pretzel family. In honor of my crazy, popcorn-less, slapstick-loving son, let's watch a comedy."

The crowd erupted in cheers and applause. Under the direction of McKell's mom, they scooted the couches back and people started filling in the floor space like kids at an elementary school assembly. I was way off on my numbers—this had to be more than fifty. We weren't going to fit very well.

If I died and my grandparents had a party for me, hardly anyone would show up. Maybe my mom, maybe not. And maybe McKell. Danny, that boy with the bald head, knew some things I hadn't figured out yet.

Someone had pulled the dining table behind the couches and people were sitting in the chairs and on the tabletop. McKell motioned for me to join her in a corner. It wasn't in front, but we could lean against a wall and still see.

I overheard some girl talking about how Danny had sent her the nicest text after she'd had the most terrible day. A boy added that Danny always called him "Mr. Fantastic." He said his coach had called him that at a game and Danny'd heard it.

The movie started and the noise died down.

The projection on the wall was huge. I saw more expression on the actors' faces than I ever remembered seeing before. I loved the separation of colors. They didn't all bleed together. And their eyes—eyes could tell a story by themselves. I didn't usually notice that. Eventually, the man in the mask chased after the princess, fighting against the sword champion until he was backed into a wall. Then the famous line: "I am not left-handed." He switched hands and started to win. I saw it coming, but laughed anyway.

McKell's arm leaned against mine a little. Had she done that on purpose? I looked over at her, but she stared forward. It was crowded and we were all a little squished together. It really wasn't a big deal. Well, I didn't think so. Okay, I wasn't sure. But probably not. But it looked like she was trying not to notice me, but she really did. That's a thing, right? Looking but not looking? And I could see it. A few weeks ago, I would have completely missed it. This new eye was incredible. If only my other one was as good.

"Thanks for coming," McKell whispered.

"Sure thing," I said. "And you already said that."

"I know," she said. It was kind of hard to hear her over the movie. She never would have said this stuff at school.

MIDDLE-SCHOOL RULE: People act differently when they don't think everyone is watching them.

"I didn't invite Gavin, and Travis, and Chloe, and Emma," she said. "I didn't want to. They wouldn't have wanted to come. This isn't exactly a popular-kid party."

I nodded. She was probably right.

"But," I said, looking around. "There are a lot of people here. Maybe Danny's just a different kind of popular."

McKell nodded and looked around.

"I need more friends like you," McKell whispered. "Like these people." She offered me the rest of her oversized pretzel and I took it.

On the screen, the man in the mask faced the giant. He must have said something funny because everyone erupted in laughter again. I missed it.

Before the noise died down, the show flicked off. In a flash, we were all staring at a blank wall in the darkness.

"What happened?" someone asked.

"Electrical problem?"

"No. I think Mr. Panganiban turned it off."

"Just posted—"

A boy in the front held up his phone. "No way! A new challenge."

A lot of mumbling and people talking over each other followed.

McKell lifted her phone and started searching it.

"Everyone," McKell's dad said loudly. "Danny just posted another challenge." He moved to the front where everyone could see him. "It's almost like he knew we were all together. Should we watch it?"

Everyone agreed. As Danny's dad hooked up his phone to the projector, the room filled with happy chattering. I heard Danny's voice from a few places as some people couldn't wait for us to watch it together and began on their phones. I would have too if I had data. Had Danny done this? Had he known we'd all be together and wanted to post it right now?

So awesome. And creepy.

After a flash of white, Danny's face appeared on the screen.

CHAPTER 20

ANOTHER CHALLENGE

"Hey, everybody," Danny said, smiling like always. "Me again. Back from the dead and stuff." He pumped his fist. "It's probably not nearly as cool to hear that the second time." He shrugged.

"Well," he continued, "I thought I'd tell you a little bit about the afterlife today. Do you want to know?" He motioned with his finger for us all to come closer to him. I leaned a little forward despite myself. I hoped McKell hadn't seen that. But it would be interesting if someone could tell me what would happen after this life.

"It's really beautiful." His face was very serious. "Flowers and friends. There's an all-you-can-eat ice cream bar and unicorns are everywhere."

What?

"Just kidding," Danny said. "I'm not going to tell you. You're going to have to wait until it's your time." He smiled wide. If there was an afterlife and I got to know about it, I imagined that I probably wouldn't learn about it on YouTube. Plus, Danny prerecorded these videos. He didn't know anything then, either.

"I hope you all had a great time watching a comedy," Danny said. "Hopefully a lot of laughter was involved. Maybe some popcorn or pretzels. Ooohh—or chocolate-covered pretzels. Man, I love those. I'm eating tons of them in heaven." He winked. "I hope you shared old memories, and made new memories. You might forget some of the conversations, but you'll always remember the people you were with."

It was true. I would always remember this. I loved having somewhere to go and people to be with that weren't my grandparents. McKell was cool to hang around.

Danny clapped his hands. "Good job, everyone."

How could this guy make videos like this? He knew he was going to die, but wanted people to get together and have fun? That wouldn't be me. I would want everyone to dress in black and send me off on a flaming barge. And all of the ladies should be crying. So much crying.

"Well, what do you think?" He spread his arms wide. "Should I leave it at that? Or should I give you another challenge?"

He put a hand to his ear and pretended to listen. People shouted for another challenge.

"I thought so," Danny answered. It was cheesy, but with Danny's enthusiasm it worked somehow. I noticed a girl dab her eyes and sniffle, but she had a huge grin on her face.

"So, I've tried to be a happy person," Danny said. The film cut to him doing all sorts of smiles and goofy faces. He pulled on the sides of his mouth. He laughed loud and high. He stuck his tongue out. I don't think anyone could watch it and not smile a little. "But I wasn't always that way. In fact, at one point I was pretty bitter about my condition, about my life." He dropped all his gestures and jokes for this part. "And when I was about to turn sixteen, I started to feel really bad. I mean, I wasn't going to be able to drive. People my age were dating more and more and though I'm a handsome devil . . ." The camera did another close-up and he winked. He was back to joking. With the same joke. And somehow we all laughed as loud as we did during the movie. "Believe it or not, not every girl in my high school was clamoring to go out with me." He threw his hands up in the air. "Crazy. I know."

"I just wanted to fit in, to be accepted, to be with people and not be the weird kid. Well, I made a friend. A good buddy named Yellow who not only hung out with me, but told me that I should quit trying to be everyone else. He said I should live life my way, do what I do." Danny gave a thumbs-up. "Thanks, Yellow. You're a great friend." And somehow, his voice was thicker, like it was covered in sincerity. "A really, really good friend."

A muffled, "You too, man," was heard off-screen.

A girl's voice from the middle of the mob shouted, "I love you, Yellow!"

From the back of the room Yellow gave a loud laugh.

"So that's when I had this crazy idea to start up a YouTube channel. Maybe I wouldn't be a student body officer, or the biggest dater, or maybe I wouldn't even make friends with everyone, but I could make videos on my time, when I felt up to it. And if people wanted to watch, they could." He spread his arms. "And look at you, you amazing people. You came and watched me."

I'd given up on trying to be like everyone else a long time ago too. That was something Danny and I had in common. And I drew comics on my own time, my way, like he did his YouTube challenges. But Danny was so much more successful at what he did than I was at what I did.

"Well, for this challenge—" The camera zoomed in. "Remember that you love me." He pointed at himself with his thumbs and wiggled his eyebrows up and down on his large forehead. "And that you really can't tell me no for this one. I mean, I went to all sorts of special effort to send you this message from the dead. You're in. You're doing this." He pumped his fists a few times.

"Without further adieu," Danny said, trying to sound French on the last word. "That was terrible. Adieu. Adieu." He tried a few more times and it just got worse. He cleared his throat. Another cut. "So apparently the French word *adieu* . . . hey, look! I said it right! . . . means good-bye but Yellow says that I'm actually trying to say *ado*, which means 'fuss, trouble, or difficulty.' Like, without further fuss or trouble, let's move on. We may or may not have just looked that up." He cleared his throat. "My bad. I'm dead. Give me a break."

That got a laugh from the crowd.

Danny shifted his position. "Without any more waiting or bad French accents, here is your challenge." His mistakes did make his videos more interesting, more real. Maybe it was okay to leave them in. "Drum roll, please." He beat the desk with his fingers, then clapped his hands in the air while making a cymbal sound. "Do something amazing you've always wanted to do, but you were too scared to try." He smiled at the camera. "That's right. I've given a challenge similar to this before, but I really, really want you to do it."

McKell gasped. "No, no, no," she repeated under her breath. She tensed her shoulders and clenched her hands together.

"Go out for the play," Danny said. "Write that story, ask out that girl, start your own YouTube channel, make those brownies—" The video cut. "I don't know . . . the brownies one was kind of weird. Who's afraid of making brownies? No one. No one should be afraid of making brownies. They should all make me some brownies." He paused to lick his small lips. "Whatever it is," Danny said, "take the plunge. Do it."

Danny's face filled the screen. "Like my little sister," he said. "Don't worry about what everyone thinks. Just show them you. Try out. Perform. You're incredible."

McKell looked over at me. Her face was pale, tears welling up in her eyes. And I wasn't the only one looking at her.

She faked a smile as the lights came on and everyone started talking to each other. Then she whispered, "I'm not doing it. I just—"

I didn't even know for sure what she was talking about. "Whatever it is," I said, "you can do it. I'll help you. Plus, we had a deal. I'll finish my comic; you'll finish Danny's challenges."

She looked at me. "The deal's off."

CHAPTER 21

EYE

I leaned over my desk, drawing Squint and Rock, trying to get my mind off of McKell. She wouldn't keep our deal, but I decided to keep mine. I had to try. Maybe she'd change her mind.

The rest of the night at the party, McKell hadn't told me what she was scared of or why she wouldn't do it. Which was terrible. The night had been so great up to that point. Why was she so determined to not do Danny's challenge? I finally had a friend—maybe—and if she didn't do the challenges, what would happen next?

"I've got to go back," Squint said, still wearing an eye patch and blasting one target after another with his light-daggers. He had made his way back to his hideout on the top floor of an abandoned skyscraper. The targets fired back at him from the other end of the room at more than one hundred mph. The target-shooter trainer was his invention.

"Nice shooting, Cyclops," Rock said and barked. "Only having one eye hasn't slowed you down." He buried his face in a pile of gravel and came up crunching a mouthful.

Squint swiveled his head back and forth. "Unless something sneaks up on me from my right side," Squint said, shooting a few more. It had taken a while for him to adjust to only one eye after his last fight with Gunn and Traz. But he did look cool in his eye patch.

Squint glanced at Rock. "Could you eat a little quieter? You sound like a Cardanian chuk chomping down a tree."

"Nope," Rock said, chewing even louder. "Good to know about the right-side thing. I'll cover it, Cyclops."

"Stop calling me that," Squint said.

"It's accurate," Rock defended.

"I could call you *Biclops*," Squint said. "Or Annoyingly Loud-Chewing Magical Rock Dog Biclops. That would be accurate too."

"Point taken," Rock said, and bit into some more gravel, chewing just as loudly. "But we can't go back to Gunn's castle the same way this time or the same thing will happen to us. We need a new plan, a new advantage." He scratched behind his rock ear for a second with his rock leg. "And we need more gravel. All this adventure has made me really hungry."

"We have to try," Squint said, blasting another target. "If we don't get the Empress back, the Oververse will fall. Any army in the known kingdoms could conquer us without her leadership and power."

"That's not the point," Rock said, spitting out a rock he didn't like. "The point is that if we go back just the two of us, you'll die. We'll both die. And I'm too awesome to die."

"You're a bunch of magical rocks," Squint said. "I don't even know if you *can* die."

"I'd rather not find out," Rock said.

"Me either," Squint said, shooting from a prone position this time. "But Diamond refuses to come with us. And she won't tell me why."

"Any theories?" Rock asked, scooting closer to Squint.

"I think she may have been a new Centurion," Squint said, rolling over onto his back and shooting over his head, his accuracy still dead-on. "That could be why she was there at the castle. Gunn and the others recruited her after they abandoned me. Maybe they were training her and she switched sides."

"But she doesn't have a cape," Rock said. "All the Centurions have capes."

"No, that would just mean that her training isn't complete," Squint said. "But what doesn't make sense is why the Empress would give her diamond powers." The Empress was the most powerful force in the Oververse, but she only gifted powers; she never used them for herself. That was why she could be kidnapped. "Why give powers to someone recruited by your captors?"

"Maybe she knew Diamond would turn on her friends to help you," Rock suggested.

"Maybe," Squint said, still shooting targets as he got to his knees. "And that's why Diamond doesn't want to go back and have to fight her friends." Squint shot a few more targets then turned his back to them and began twisting around in time to shoot them.

"Or maybe there's something else she's afraid of," Rock said.

"Maybe," Squint said, and shut down the targets. He moved his hand toward his eye patch, then pulled it away. "My eye itches so bad."

"Just scratch it with your back foot, like this," Rock said, demonstrating.

"Thanks for the advice," Squint said, resting the patch on his forehead for a little relief.

His eye made a sizzling sound, followed by a spark. A glowing ember hit the floor and fizzled out.

"What was that?" Rock asked. "Did that spark just fall from your eye?"

Squint put a hand to his eye. "I think so."

"It's like you're crying fireworks," Rock said.

Squint nodded. "I felt it, too. And it's freaking me out."

Though I was really far behind, the story was coming along better than I expected. But I needed time to finish.

"Flint," Grandma said.

I didn't answer. I'd draw a little more, then I'd talk to her.

"Do you think that's a side effect of the magical surgery?" Rock asked.

"I guess so," Squint said. "But it was an actual spark."

"Flint," Grandma repeated, standing in the doorway with a serving spoon in one hand and rubbing her forehead with the other. "Sweet thing, can't you answer your grandmother the first time for once in your comic-obsessed life?"

"Um, sorry," I apologized.

"Have you written that letter yet?"

"What letter?"

"To the family of the person who gave you your eye," she said. "Remember?"

"Oh, yeah," I said. I wanted to write the letter. Say thank you. But every time I tried, I got stuck. It was just so awkward. What was I going to say? *Hey, sorry about your dead relative. This eye is cool.* Someone actually had to die for me to get this eye. Would the family even *want* a letter from me?

She put her hands on her hips. "Yeah, you wrote it?" she asked. "Or yeah, you're just remembering?"

"I'm just remembering," I admitted. "But I don't know what to write." Nothing sounded good enough.

"Tell them your story," she said. "Whoever it is, they just lost someone they loved. They might need to know something good has come of it. Get me a solid first try and I'll help you with it if you want."

I thought about giving excuses: Danny's challenge, finishing a comic that I'd started over, doing my actual homework. But it wouldn't help. Grandma wasn't going to back down. "Okay," I said.

"Okay, you'll do it right now?" she asked. "Or should I go and get Grandpa so he can tell you a story about perseverance?"

She really wasn't letting me out of this.

"I'll do it now," I gave in.

"Thank you," Grandma said. "Bring it to me when you're done." She disappeared back into the hall.

I leaned back in my seat. I didn't want to write the letter. Squint and Rock were trying to figure out Diamond and mount their final attack on Gunn and the others. But I sighed and opened a blank document.

Hello,

Good start.

> *My name is Flint and I am thirteen years old. My grandma is making me write you a letter. And seriously, she's never going to leave me alone until I do.*

Okay. I deleted the part about Grandma. She *was* going to proofread it, after all. And it didn't sound very sincere or grateful. I *was* really grateful—I just didn't know how to write it.

> *My name is Flint and I am thirteen years old. I*
> *wanted to write you a letter to tell you thank you. I've*
> *had problems with my eyes for more than three years*
> *now. Thanks to the cornea I got from someone you*
> *love, I can see so much better. Thank you.*
> *My grandpa says that saying thank you is a . . .*

Nope. I deleted that line. They wouldn't care what my grandpa says.

> *Well, I understand that you're probably going*
> *through a really hard time right now. Someone you*
> *love has died and I can't imagine what that would*
> *feel like.*

I had tried imagining what it had been like when McKell lost Danny. I could barely even grasp what someone would feel. They were probably like McKell's family—sad, but trying to get by. How would they feel if they got a letter like this? Would it help?

They could get a letter like this. Danny had only been dead for a few weeks. If he was a donor . . .

My heart thudded. He died in the last few weeks. If he . . .

My fingers clicked the keys as I looked up Danny's

CHAD MORRIS & SHELLY BROWN

obituary again. When did he die? When did he die? There it was. I checked my calendar. It was a week before my surgery. My fingers typed in a flurry. *How long after someone dies would a cornea be okay to use for a transplant?*

I scrolled through the answers. Up to fourteen days.

It could be him.

Wait. He had a disease. They wouldn't give me the cornea of someone who had a disease, right? What was his condition called? I checked his obituary. Progeria. A few searches later I found out that unless he had active cancer or some other serious diseases, he would have been able to donate his corneas. So maybe . . .

I took a deep breath. There was a chance I was staring through Danny's eye right now.

CHAPTER 22

BUZZ

"Hey, McKell," I said, catching up to her as we left science class. We'd just learned about meiosis, mitosis's cousin, and my brain hurt. "Can I talk to you?"

"Squint," she said, holding her books in front of her. "Hey." She grinned, but then it faded away.

I searched her eyes. Was this okay? Was it not? We had gotten along so well at her house, but now we were back in school. It didn't seem like she hated talking to me, so I kept going. "I wanted to talk about meiosis some more," I said.

She raised an eyebrow.

"I'm kidding," I said. "Bad joke." I cleared my throat. "I know you said that you didn't want to do Danny's challenge, but I don't even know what he wants you to do. Maybe I could help and stuff." And stuff? That was awkward. But I couldn't stop thinking that if Danny were here, he would want to help. And maybe I was looking through his eye. Maybe I could see better than anyone else that she needed help.

But I wasn't sure I should tell her about the eye thing.

We were coming up on the door to the hallway. I didn't know whether to follow her again or not.

We walked out into the hall. She wasn't running away from me or anything. In fact, after a few more steps, it was like we were walking together on purpose. And this was the second time.

"It's just terrifying," she said.

"What's terrifying?" I asked.

She shook her head.

"I was up until midnight last night working on my comic," I said. "That diamond girl is working out amazing. She was a great idea. And it's good for me to draw even when I don't want to. It's like an escape, even though I'm still not sure I'm good enough. And I'm sure whatever you're supposed to do would be great too, if—"

"I would try out for the school talent show," she said quietly.

It took me a second to realize what she had said. "That's what you've always wanted to do? That's what Danny wants you to do?" Maybe I had Danny's eye, but I didn't see that coming.

"Well," she said, "something like it. Perform somewhere."

"Great," I said. "What would you do? I mean, perform?"

She looked at me, choosing her words carefully. "Sing a song I wrote."

"A song?" I asked. "That's great. You're amazing at rhyming so I'm sure the words will be great. Would you play the . . . the—" I remembered she had mentioned some instrument with a weird name. I couldn't come up with it.

"The uke?" she asked.

"That's it," I said. The small guitar that sounded like a hairy animal.

She looked around a little, and her mind was spinning. I don't know how I could tell. Maybe it was because I could see better, or maybe Danny's eye gave me special abilities. "Look, Squint, I'd better go." She said it almost like a question.

I looked down the hall and saw Emma and Chloe talking to each other where the next hallway crossed. Okay. So she was still figuring out how much she wanted to be seen with me. "Wait," I said. "I wanted to ask you something else."

"I'm not changing my mind," she said.

This wasn't working. And I doubted I could convince her while she was worried about Chloe and Emma. "Can we just talk at lunch? Or after school?" If she didn't want anyone to see us together, I could meet her somewhere. We could go hiking again.

She thought for a moment, then pulled out her phone. "What's your number?"

I almost choked. My number? A girl was asking for my number. And a popular girl?

McKell looked down the hall then repeated the question.

I rattled off my number and she plugged it into her phone. Then she walked away.

I watched her fiddle with her phone as she met up with Chloe and Emma. A moment later my pocket buzzed and there was a text.

> McKell

It was just her name, but it was the first time I'd gotten a text that wasn't from my mom or my grandparents. I wasn't ever going to delete it. And it meant I had her number too.

Now I had to figure out what to text the first girl I ever texted. And how to convince her to do something that terrified her.

CHAPTER 23

TEXTING

Hey

Sorry I couldn't talk in the hall.

It's okay.

She wasn't sure how much she wanted to be seen hanging out with the comic kid, but she gave me her number. In some ways, that was better than walking together in the halls. And she was actually answering as I texted from my corner table at lunch. So far, so good.

Any chance I can hear your song?

No answer. Did I ask too soon? Did I break some texting rule?

> It wouldn't take long, to hear your song. I'm probably not wrong. #badrhyming

It wasn't very clever, but it was the best idea I could think of.

> No way, not any day, in May, September, October, or June, no time soon. #noway #inrhyme

At least she answered. I looked over at her table and she glanced back at me and raised her eyebrow. Maybe there was even a bit of a smile. Rhyming always seemed to help.

> Great rhyming. Not a great answer.

> Performing is terrifying. 😩😩😩😩

> Terrifying 😫😫😫

> Seriously 😱😱😱

> I'm fine playing just for me, but when everyone is looking at me, my brain freaks out.

> It would be scary.

And it would be. I couldn't imagine doing it. I could barely let anyone see my comic.

> If I play a song I wrote it's even scarier. It's like sharing me.

> And people don't always like me.

Did people always text like this? I wasn't sure she would say what she texted to me face to face. I'm sure there are texting rules that I had no idea about.

> What? Sure they do.

> At my last school not everyone liked me.

> If that's true, they're total dorks. They don't know you well enough.

I thought that was a pretty good thing to say. But she didn't text back for the rest of lunch. So, maybe not.

I looked over and saw Gavin, Travis, Chloe, and Emma all talking with her. Maybe they were asking about who she was texting. Maybe she couldn't pretend it was someone else anymore.

But I did see her glance over at my table again. That was good, right?

Just before my next class, it started up again. Which felt awesome. I'd never had my phone buzzing like other kids as I sat down at my desk.

> I don't think people would like it. Can you imagine Gavin and Chloe liking any song on the ukulele?

> Not sure. But who cares if they like it?

> I do. Maybe I shouldn't, but I do.

Again. Super honest.

> I'm sure I'd love it.

> You're not going to see it.

> Please. Just me. No crowd. One person who doesn't really matter at school.

> You matter.

> Sorry. I didn't realize I texted that.

And I hadn't realized it. I wasn't looking for her pity. I was just trying to mention that showing something to me wasn't that big of a deal. But I still really liked her answer.

Mr. Daniels stood up and started class.

Grandma always said that I should never text during class, but I really couldn't help it. I tried to keep my phone below my desk.

> Could you play for Danny?

> Yeah. Toward the end I could. He would say that I was amazing and that I really needed to show people.

> Toward the end? Not always?

"Mr. Flint," Mr. Daniels said. "Would you please put your phone away and pay attention?"

Busted. I shoved it deep in my pocket.

Buzz.

Buzz.

Buzz.

Three times. McKell was still texting. Maybe she was better at hiding it. Or maybe she was in a class where a teacher didn't care. But it was driving me crazy. Who can focus on extending your vocabulary when your pocket is buzzing? Especially when

McKell just said that she couldn't always play for Danny. He seemed like one of the nicest people ever.

I pulled it out and took another glance.

> Danny wasn't always fun. I didn't always like him. He always got tons of attention because of his looks. Some people pointed and stared. Some joked. But I felt invisible. I know that's selfish, but it's how I felt.

> I just wanted people to notice me. Danny didn't notice. He was too worried about himself. And he had a lot of problems so that made sense.

> Then he made a few friends. Like Yellow. And he changed. When he knew people liked him, he was different.

Whoa. I hadn't thought of any of that. I guess friends can make a big difference. But I was too chicken to text back after Mr. Daniels had busted me once, so I put my phone away.

After class, I pulled it out. McKell hadn't said anything else so I responded about friends.

That's cool.
#Friends

I wasn't entirely sure what that meant but I wanted her to know that I had gotten her messages.

I didn't dare touch my phone during my last class. Mr. Gardner would stomp it to dust if he caught me. McKell texted again while I was in line for the bus. I'd received more texts in a day than I'd gotten over the last month combined.

After he had friends, Danny noticed me more. But I still didn't want to do his challenges. #bitter. He was getting attention and I wasn't. #jealous. But eventually he won me over.

I didn't know what to send back. Texting wasn't like comic writing. Once I sent it, I couldn't change it, make it better.

Sorry he's gone.

I hoped that was a good thing to say.

Me too. I just wish I could be like him. I think he recorded these last challenges to help me.

> What can I do to help?

I stepped onto the bus. And then I was that kid who was texting the whole ride. And it actually went okay.

> Maybe I'll show you my song. On 3 conditions.

> AWESOME!!!!

> 1) You have to promise not to laugh.

> Done. Why would I laugh?

> Because it might be stupid and immature and not very good.

> Danny liked it. So will I.

> He never heard this one. It's new.

> Okay. But he would like it if he heard it.

> After he changed, he liked everything.

Okay, then no one else matters. You can do it for him, right?

But you're still going to hear it.

Yeah. But it's for him. If you go to a birthday party, all the other people there don't have to like what you give the birthday boy. Just him. You do it for him and you'll be fine. If others like it, then it's like bonus points.

😆 I like that.

Good. What are your other conditions?

2) You show me your comic. The whole thing so I understand what's going on in the story.

My insides tightened. Nobody had seen my entire comic. I'd been working like crazy and I had made some hefty changes, but I didn't know if it was good enough yet. I swallowed hard. Really hard. I remembered Gavin reading parts and mocking it. And Chloe dropping it like it was a piece of scratch paper. But McKell had already seen some of it and liked what she'd seen. Plus, I guessed I'd have to show her something that was part of me for her to risk showing me part of her.

"Texting your grandma?" a voice asked.

Gavin. Of course. He was always on the bus.

"Yep." I tilted the screen away from him. There was no way I was going to tell him who I was really texting.

He grinned big for a second and then tried to nab my phone. And he was fast. Thankfully I'd thought he might try that and had turned to the side, protecting my phone with the rest of my body. It would be terrible if he read our messages. Disastrous. McKell would hate it. I wasn't going to let that happen.

He pulled on me, trying to turn me around. Despite leaning away as hard as I could, Gavin was strong. I tightened my grip on my phone, my fingers turning a little white. But I knew he could wrestle it away from me. He was bigger and stronger. It would be like Mantis trying to keep something away from Thanos.

"Hey, settle down back there," the bus driver said. "And sit down."

Gavin tried again.

"Sit down," the driver repeated.

He was one of my favorite people in existence in that moment.

Gavin sat.

I double-checked that he was far away before texting back.

> Okay. I can bring my comic tomorrow.

But when was McKell going to read it? Was she going to carry around my portfolio at school where everyone would see? Doubt it. Take it home? Again, it didn't seem likely.

> Or I could show you now. I could walk to your place. Or meet somewhere.

Was that stupid? Did I seem desperate?

I checked Gavin again. He was pretending to text someone and making stupid-looking faces to make fun of me. I didn't care.

> Today? Maybe. But it makes more sense for me to come over to your place. That's where the comic is, right?

Maybe? Really? Maybe?

But my place? That's not what I had proposed. It made sense, but I couldn't have McKell over at my house. Her house was all nice. Mine was . . . not even close. I didn't even have normal parents. I had brought Gavin over a long time ago and he had called it a shack that smelled like old people. And that was when we got along.

> Nah. Let's meet somewhere else.

I deleted it before I sent it. McKell was actually going to show me her song if I did this.

> Okay. Here's my address.

I typed my address in.

> Cool. If I can, I'll come by in a little while.

So crazy. I never thought this would happen.

> And the third condition?

> We both agree that this doesn't mean that I'm showing my song to anyone else.

> Okay.

I hoped this wasn't going to all blow up in my face.

CHAPTER 24

MY HOUSE

I didn't have time to mow the lawn. Because of Grandpa's back, it was my job and, as usual, it looked terrible. But McKell texted that she was on her way. I only had a few minutes.

So I tried to pick up any garbage lying around, roll up the hose, and push anything else out of sight around the side of the house. Of course, the Hulk wanted some attention while I was outside, so I let him run around.

The neighbor's Chihuahuas must have spotted us because they started yapping through their front window. The Hulk barked back. This could go on forever.

What a great first impression. I glanced up the road to see if she was coming.

I had looked at this street a million times, but this time I saw it with different eyes. And I'm not talking about Danny's cornea. My neighborhood wasn't nearly as nice as McKell's. I noticed every rickety mailbox, every weedy lawn, every junker car in a driveway. And of course the houses were a lot smaller. Flat and simple patterns. Run-down and old. Even the roads weren't as well maintained.

And coming down the center of it was McKell on a dark red mountain bike. It looked expensive. She slowed and jumped off as she reached my driveway.

"I've never been in this neighborhood," she said, panting and looking around.

"I know it's kind of junky," I admitted.

"No," she said, "just older. I bet when these houses were built this was the coolest place to live. Close to the middle school. Close to the library. Close to the McDonald's."

I chuckled. But McDonald's made me think of my mom. She had texted me again and said that she would take me out to eat sometime this week and catch up. We'd probably go to McDonald's. If it ever happened.

"Come on in," I said, hoping to ease the embarrassment by getting her away from the unmowed lawn. At least Grandma kept flowers planted along the house.

I opened the door and stepped in. Grandpa had the afternoon shift, so I didn't have to worry about him. At least no one would try to tell McKell any super-long football stories. But I could hear water running in the kitchen. I had poked my head in and told Grandma that a friend would be coming. She seemed excited. I wanted to ask her not to embarrass me, but that would have probably backfired on me, so I didn't bother.

"You don't have to take off your shoes," I explained as we came in. McKell had started to slip them off. The carpet was like fifty years old and for the first time in my life I realized I could smell it. Dusty, musty. I wanted to apologize and send McKell home.

The water stopped and Grandma came in the front room. "I thought I heard voices. Flint, who is this?" She reached out her hand.

"This is McKell," I said.

"Very nice to meet you," Grandma said. "And aren't you prettier than socks on a rooster?"

"That's a good thing," I assured McKell. "This is my grandma, Elizabeth." I hoped my face didn't turn red. My grandma had her same wispy appearance and hadn't changed out of her Holiday Inn uniform yet.

"Nice to meet you," McKell said. If she was disgusted, she didn't show it.

"We're just going to grab something," I said, "in my room." I pointed down the hall. I could see Grandma's mouth open so I beat her to it. "We'll leave the door open." She nodded her approval and I pulled McKell out of the front room and down the hall.

My room.

I hadn't checked my room. What did it look like? Maybe McKell should stay in the kitchen with Grandma and I could bring the comic out to her. But I'd already said we'd be going to my room. I kept leading the way.

I panicked when I saw my clothes from yesterday on the edge of the bed. I grabbed them as quickly as possible as we walked in, but felt something under my foot. I looked down and saw I was standing on yesterday's underwear.

"Where are your parents?" McKell asked.

I threw my clothes in the open hamper across the room. "Um." It's crazy that I've answered this question my whole life and it still feels awkward every time. "My dad left before I was born. I don't know him at all. And my mom isn't very good at being a mom. So my mom's parents are kind of like my parents."

I sat on the edge of the bed, trying very hard to hook my underwear with the toe of my shoe without being too obvious about it.

She sat on my bed and I was so grateful that Grandma had me make my bed that morning. For once I was glad I'd done my chores. "You live with your grandparents? Cool. Your grandma seems nice."

I glanced down quickly. *Got it!* I slowly brought my foot up like I was going to sit cross-legged and pulled my underwear off my toe and wadded it up into an unrecognizable ball in my hand.

"When she's not being bossy," I said, walking to the hamper this time. I didn't want to miss and have my underwear flop all over the floor.

"She didn't seem bossy," McKell said. "Besides, most

parents are bossy. It's part of being a parent. If they just gave you money and made your meals they'd be your bank and restaurant, not your parents." She laughed a little. She'd probably gotten that from an adult.

I doubt I'd hear anyone say anything like that at school. Not even McKell.

MIDDLE-SCHOOL RULE: Cool kids don't defend parents—or teachers.

I moved from the hamper to my desk and grabbed a stack of papers. "This is it. It's stupid," I said handing her my comic. "And some of the art is bad. I couldn't see well with my eyes and my glasses didn't help enough." The words sounded pathetic as they tumbled out.

McKell grabbed her end of the stack of papers but I couldn't let go of mine. What if she thought it was awful and told everyone? I mean, I already knew that it had problems. "I can see how bad it is now that I have my good eye. So I might not enter it into the contest." More rambling.

I let go and took a step back. "Either way it won't win. It's not finished, not entirely. The ending has more—"

She shushed me. "Stop talking so I can read."

I put my back against the wall and watched for a minute. When she flipped the first page I slid down the wall and sat with my arms wrapped around my knees. I felt wound up, like my insides were stuffed into a space only half as big as it should be.

She laughed and I knew exactly what joke that was.

She flipped through a few more pages and gasped and chuckled in all of the right places. At one point she looked up from the comic to see me just sitting there staring at her. I'm sure I had a big dumb smile on my face.

"I'll go get us a snack or something," I said, jumping to my feet. I didn't want to sit there awkwardly watching her as she read.

She nodded.

My grandma was in the kitchen working on dinner when I got there. Her old laptop was open on the counter. She must have been looking up a recipe. "You look as happy as Grandpa when Big Red wins."

I didn't know what to say to that.

Grandma smiled. "She seems real nice."

"She is," I said.

"Grandpa would want me to tell you to treat her really well," Grandma said. "And he would tell you some story of someone who didn't treat some woman well and how shameful it was."

I nodded. "I'll pretend he told me the stories and I'll live by them." I peered in the pantry. "Can I make a snack?" I asked.

"It's almost dinn—" Grandma didn't finish. She looked at me for a moment then glanced down the hall. "Yes," she said.

Once I got back, I felt embarrassed that all I had were cracker sandwiches. But I'd said I would get a snack so I had to come back with something. McKell took one from the plate. "It's good," she said.

"It's just peanut butter and saltines," I said.

"I meant the comic," she said. "It's really, really good," she corrected, nodding to accentuate her point.

"It's not as good as it should be," I said.

"Are you kidding me?" she asked. "I think it's great." And she emphasized *great*. "I mean, look at this." She held up a page with Squint soaring and fighting against Gunn. "This looks fantastic. The colors are fun, the characters are interesting, and I love where this story is going. You could make people pay to read this kind of stuff." Her voice was a little louder. I tried to figure out if she was really as excited as she seemed.

"No way," I said. "Not even close." My cheeks felt hot.

"Well, to you, maybe," McKell said. "But not to me. I can't figure out what they're going to do next. It's so interesting." She made me wonder if I was too critical of myself and my story. "But the best part is this Diamond girl. Whoever came up with her was brilliant."

I laughed. "A straight-up genius. For sure."

McKell's voice got a little softer. "I hope she ends up helping Squint out."

"Me too," I said.

Neither of us said anything else for a moment.

"He had to squint to get a glint," McKell started, bobbing her head with her beat. "And put in his heart to start, but now with his new eye, he tried, and the new comic . . ." She paused, her eyes looking to the side. "The new comic . . . the new comic," she repeated.

"Yeah, good luck rhyming that," I said, trying to think of options and not coming up with anything.

"Oh, I can rhyme with it," she said. "Just nothing good. Balsamic. Economic. 'The new comic is economic' doesn't sound very cool, you know?" She turned her hands up. "Wait. Got it." She stood up straighter. "With his new eye, he tried, and the new comic is . . . atomic." She nodded in approval and then made an exploding noise.

"It's a good thing to have an atomic comic, right?" I asked.

"Definitely," she said. "You might just win this contest."

"Thanks," I said. "There really isn't much of a chance, plus I'm going to have to work like crazy to finish it."

"You might surprise yourself," she said.

I wanted to bring up our deal, the challenges, but I didn't. "Maybe," I said.

She looked down. "Oh, yeah. Now it's my turn."

CHAPTER 25

MISS

McKell decided to get it over with. Even though Grandma said dinner was in an hour, we biked to her house. And of course my bike squeaked every time I pushed on the left pedal.

The houses on her street had so much detail. Brick, stone, and wood placed just right, with windows of all shapes and sizes, spires and gables on the roofs. Definitely something I wouldn't have noticed before I got my new eye.

I recognized McKell's home and we dropped our bikes and made our way up the front walkway, past the fountain that wasn't turned on, and in through the huge front doors. The house was quiet except the ticking of some clock in another part of the room. It was interesting to see where the furniture usually sat when the place wasn't set up for a movie party. It

reminded me of a house on TV. Very fancy, like nobody actually lived there. Like a waiting room at the doctor's office.

We slipped off our shoes again. Thankfully, my socks didn't
have holes in them. "Have a seat," McKell said, gesturing toward the fancy family room. "I'll get my ukulele and be back."
She disappeared down the hall and I sat down on a large brown
leather chair.

"Hello, there," a voice said from the kitchen. McKell's
mom was so quiet I didn't see her sitting in her pajamas at the
table with a mug and a book. "What are you kids up to?"

A grown-up in her pajamas at dinnertime? Odd. Maybe
she was going to bed early. Maybe she had some appointment
really early in the morning.

"I'm Squi—I mean Flint," I said. "I was here the other
night for the movie," I rambled, sitting a little straighter and
fidgeting with my hands. "McKell is going to show me one of
her songs."

Her mother's face lit up. "Really?"

I nodded. "At least, she told me she would."

McKell came in the room holding her ukulele. "Mom!" she
nearly shouted when she noticed her mother in the kitchen.
She shuddered and grabbed my hand. "That's it. We're going
outside."

Her mother gave a tired smile as McKell dragged me into
the backyard. "I'm really sorry about her. There's not much
more embarrassing than a mom that hasn't got out of her pajamas."

Oh. McKell's mom hadn't gotten into her pajamas early; she hadn't changed out of them. "Don't worry about it. She's fine," I said. I had never seen that before. My grandparents were always up and dressed before I was really awake.

McKell looked at me and shook her head.

Hadn't we just done this at my place? I was embarrassed by my grandma, but McKell wasn't. Now we had switched.

MIDDLE-SCHOOL RULE: Every kid thinks their parents are embarrassing. (But mine really are.)

I could see McKell's mother from where she sat, looking out a big kitchen window at us. "My grandma's hair is fake blonde and she was wearing her work uniform."

McKell suppressed a smile. "Your grandma was really nice. My mom's depressed. She can't even be a mom right now."

I swallowed hard. A mom who couldn't be a mom was something I knew too well. Probably a lot more than McKell.

"Sorry," was all I said. I couldn't help but glance once more at her mom, who was still watching from the window and holding her mug with both hands.

It was time to change the subject, I could sense it. I gave her a big smile. "Let's hear your song."

She nodded, sat against the patio table, took a deep breath, and began strumming. I pulled a chair out so I could watch her.

Strumming.

And more strumming.

She wasn't saying or singing anything, just strumming. Was she chickening out?

"I'll love it," I said. "Promise."

She looked down at her moving fingers. "It's not as good as your comic."

I chuckled. "It's probably better. Just play already."

McKell stopped her strumming and ran her fingers through her hair. She shuffled the position of her ukulele and glanced towards the kitchen window, which was now empty.

She started again and eventually her voice came out, breathy and light.

"Miss. Miss. Miss," she sang. "Miss. Miss. Miss."

Please like it. Please like it. Please like it. I really didn't want to have to fake anything. I wasn't very good at faking.

Her voice became fuller, each note right on pitch. The last note she even moved it up and down like singers on the radio. She sounded good and the ukulele blended right in.

"Miss," she drew out the word, long and lonely before going into her first verse.

> *You can miss a train or the rain, or your chance to*
> *explain.*
> *You can misspell, mismatch, miss your love, miss a*
> *catch.*

Her words had a beat and melody that moved along well together.

> *Miss a chance for romance,*

Miss it all by happenstance.
Misjudge, mistreat, miss the turn down the street.

She changed rhythms, longer, and slower.

Don't misunderstand.
You can miss all that you've planned,

The strumming calmed. She closed her eyes.

And I can miss a smile.
I can miss a laugh.
And all of this missing, feels like I'm only half
The person I once knew.

She paused and sang beautifully soft, a little quiver in her voice.

I miss you.

Obviously, it was about Danny. Did I have any clue what it must be like for her? I had lost my mom—kinda. I didn't really have her in my life. And some days that felt really terrible. But she wasn't dead. I would see her again. I didn't even know my dad, so it didn't feel like I had lost anything. I had lost friends, like Gavin and the other boys I used to play with, but again, they weren't dead. Losing Danny would be a million times harder.

"It's really good," I whispered while she strummed a few parts without words. She seemed to relax a little.

The song went on with a few more verses and a longer chorus at the end. There was no way around it, McKell was talented. Her rhymes were clever and her voice was hypnotizing. And I had never heard anything like it. She had a style all her own.

"Really, really good," I said, when it was all done. "And it's so you. The way you rhyme and everything."

"Thanks," she said, a little red on her tan cheeks. "Danny kept telling me to make my songs more like me and less like the songs on the radio."

"Well, it sounded like you," I said. "And I'd put it on the radio." I looked away for a moment. "I'm sorry that you miss him so much."

She nodded.

"But I guess that's also a huge compliment to him," I said. "You really loved him. If you didn't, you wouldn't miss him so badly."

She nodded again. "I guess you're right."

"You should totally do it," I said.

"What?" she said.

"The song. You should sing it in the talent assembly. I mean . . . um, you should try out. And then they'll definitely pick you and *then* you should sing it in the assembly."

She dropped her head. "I still can't do it. It is one thing to sing in front of one person and a whole different thing to sing for hundreds of people who aren't sure they want to listen to you."

"You're totally right," I said. "At least I think you are. I haven't sung in front of anybody since our third-grade 'America Is Great' program." I brought my hand to my chest.

McKell set down her ukulele on the table and chuckled.

She had to do this. I wasn't going to let it go until she agreed. "But can you imagine how happy that would make Danny for you to show everyone what you can do?"

"Maybe," she said.

"When are tryouts?"

"Thursday," she said. "They've been announcing them for weeks."

"Right," I said again. "I should probably pay attention to announcements. I tend to tune them out." I punched my open hand. "You can do this." Maybe it sounded cheesy. If it were a line in my comic I would try to think of something more original, but I meant it. And that was enough for now.

She looked up. Her voice trembling, she said, "Maybe."

CHAPTER 26

AUDITIONS

I sat in the back row of the auditorium watching five girls dance. The two in the middle were Chloe and Emma. And they were good. They moved and swayed and swished the way good dancers did.

And Chloe looked as cute as ever. I swear all of the boys at school liked her. Well, like 95 percent of them. But not me. At least not like I used to.

McKell hadn't showed up yet, but I still hoped she would. She had actually signed up. I told her I'd be waiting for her. Maybe she could come in and sit a few rows in front of me. That way she wouldn't have to be seen with me, but she could still know I was there for support. It wasn't my favorite situation, but what else was I going to do?

"Hey." I turned and saw McKell. She had her ukulele in a case at her side. She sat down right next to me. "Can I sit here?"

I looked up at Chloe and Emma on stage and then back at her. "Sure, if you want."

"I think I'm going to need it," she said. Her voice trembled a little.

McKell Panganiban actually came to tryouts, and she was sitting right next to me.

Right next to me.

And Emma and Chloe could totally see. I didn't know if they'd notice. They were kind of busy right now. But they could.

Today was going to be life-changing. McKell would make it into the talent show and I would finish up my comic and send it in tomorrow. I still wasn't confident in it, but I could try.

At the last note, the dancing girls all froze in different dramatic poses. Everyone clapped. McKell joined in, so I gave a few claps too. Mine weren't very loud.

"Great job," Mrs. Lin, the drama teacher said. Mr. Mueller, the choir director, sat front and center, the tryout list in his hand.

"Well done," Mr. Mueller said. Then he turned out to the auditorium with students waiting to perform. He glanced at the list. "Caleb Hein is up next. JanaLee Gonzalez to follow."

Chloe, Emma, and the other girls all hugged and

congratulated each other. Then they grabbed duffel bags, probably filled with their non-dancing clothes, and walked up the aisle toward the doors. They were going to walk right past us.

They were still talking with each other and I hoped they wouldn't notice us.

Chloe stopped. "Hey, McKell."

"Good job, girls," McKell said. I couldn't tell if it bothered her that they noticed her or not.

"Yeah, thanks," Emma added. Then she looked at me and back at McKell. I could almost see her mind working. Why were we sitting together?

"Is there something wrong with your eye?" Chloe asked, looking at me. Weird question, but I was glad it wasn't something like, "What are you doing here together?" or "Why don't you go hang out with people on your level?"

The other girls all looked at my eye. "It's really red," McKell said. "Is it okay?" I guess she hadn't noticed it before.

I shrugged and blinked several times. It was irritated and dry, but that happened. "I'll put in some drops after auditions."

Chloe looked back at McKell. "What is . . . Wait, are you two trying out?"

I shook my head and pointed at McKell.

McKell took a deep breath. "I am. Well, at least I think so."

"What are you going to do?" Emma asked.

McKell lifted her ukulele case. "Just playing and singing a little."

"She's really good," I said. It just slipped out.

All of a sudden I realized the implications of what I'd said. It meant that I knew something about McKell that they didn't. That meant that I had spent time with her outside of school and that she showed me something that she hadn't shown them. I had given a lot away with one stupid sentence. I wished it was in a comic so I could erase it and shut up.

"Thanks." McKell smiled at me. I didn't know whether to be terrified that Emma and Chloe had seen McKell and me sitting together—or thrilled that McKell seemed fine with it.

Chloe looked at me and then McKell and then at Emma. Her face looked a little confused. "Well, we've got to go. Good luck." She pointed at my eye. "You might want to have that looked at."

"Break a leg," Emma said. "Or whatever they say when you're about to sing."

And then they left. I didn't know what to think about that. They didn't mock her. That was good. But shouldn't they have stayed? Watched their friend? Maybe they had somewhere they had to be. Of course, I was pretty glad they didn't stick around.

I worried that they were going to tease McKell about this later. About hanging out with me. About singing with a ukulele in the talent show.

On stage, a yo-yo flew away from Caleb's hand then zoomed over his shoulder and back in front of him. Pretty cool. I did have to blink a little extra. Maybe my eye was drier than normal.

McKell tapped her fingernails on the ukulele across her lap.

Beside me. At school. I was still surprised.

"You okay?" I asked.

"Terrified," she said, tapping faster. She had seemed so confident talking with Chloe and Emma a couple of minutes ago. Now she was practically trembling. Maybe it was because it was getting closer. Maybe she needed to be distracted or something.

"He's good," I said, nodding toward Caleb.

"Yeah," she said, not really looking at him. She eyed the exit door a few rows back. Was she regretting coming? Did she want to run and catch up to Chloe and Emma and tell them she had just been joking?

Caleb finished with several giant whirls and catching the yo-yo. Everyone clapped. Mrs. Lin called up JanaLee Gonzalez and she approached a piano on the side of the stage. I closed my eye to give it just a bit of a break. JanaLee started to play something calm and peaceful. Good timing. I hoped it might relax McKell.

"Maybe it was good enough that I came this far," McKell mumbled. "I've never even sat in a room waiting to audition. Danny would understand."

"Maybe," I whispered back. JanaLee played a little louder. "But I don't understand. You're really good, McKell. Plus, you rock the ukulele. Well, if anyone can rock a ukulele. It seems like a weird thing to say. But you're really good."

She let out a quiet laugh, but it was still a little too loud.

"You've got this," I said.

She looked back at the exit sign.

I tried to reassure her by patting her forearm, but she grabbed my hand and clutched it tight. "No, I don't," she said. Her hand trembled a little. It was like I was a lifeline and she couldn't let go. This was not what I'd thought my first experience holding hands with a girl would be like. It was more of a death grip. I squeezed back, trying to reassure her and hoping it didn't come across as too awkward.

We saw three more acts: a monologue about someone's father dying (super dramatic), a juggler, and someone who sang "The Star-Spangled Banner" while pogo-sticking. Which was weird, but cool.

McKell's clutching and fidgeting just got worse.

"McKell Panganiban," Mr. Mueller, the choir director, finally called out in his deep voice. He always spoke like he was in a play.

McKell swallowed. Her face reminded me of the squirrels that the Hulk liked to corner in the backyard. She let go of my hand and stumbled trying to get out to the aisle.

I didn't know what to do, so I did the only thing I could think of. "McKell, will do well," I rhymed. "And cast a spell over all of us, like a . . ."

McKell's look of confusion suddenly gave way to a nervous smile. "A school bus? A fuss? A little phosphorus? You need to think it through a little more." She shook her head as she walked away. If nothing else, she made it all of the way up to the stage.

McKell walked quickly and nervously to the center of the stage. She mumbled into the microphone, "I'm McKell Panganiban and I'm going to sing a song that I wrote."

Part of her was blurry. Dumb dry red eye. I took off my glasses and rubbed my temples. I clenched my eyes shut and then opened them. Still blurry.

McKell adjusted her ukulele. This was it. Danny wanted her to do this and she'd finally found the guts to do it. Soon everyone would know how talented she was. Then she would be on the trail to becoming famous. She'd feel more confident. Like she was becoming the type of person her brother wanted her to be.

She raised her hand and gave a few strums. I tried to blink away the blurriness. It must have been a headache setting in. She strummed a few more times.

She was about to start singing in three, two . . .

A few more strums.

I must have been off. The words were coming now.

But she never said them. She opened her mouth, then ran across the stage behind the curtain.

Oh, no. What was wrong?

Then we heard it. An unmistakable sound.

Throwing up.

My heart dive-bombed. No. This wasn't the way it was supposed to go.

A few boys in the crowd snickered, but I jumped out of my
chair and ran up to the stage and behind the curtain. With my
weird blurry sight and my headache, I almost missed a stair.

Thankfully, there had been a garbage can back there and
McKell had made it. She still had her face buried in it.

"Are you okay?" I asked.

"Go away," she said, a mix between trying to catch her
breath and crying.

"McKell, I'm sorry," Mrs. Lin said. Apparently, she had followed me backstage. "Is there anything you need?"

"No," McKell said, her voice echoing through the bottom
of the can. She looked up at Mrs. Lin. "I'll dump this when
I'm done."

"Are you sure?" Mrs. Lin asked. "Maybe take a few deep
breaths and—"

"Just keep going," McKell interrupted, turning back to the
garbage.

The drama teacher nodded. "Okay, but you can still audition when you feel better." She patted McKell and as she
turned to leave, she glanced at me. "Is your eye okay?" Mrs.
Lin asked.

I nodded.

She looked again and then left the stage. It was better that
way. Less attention to McKell.

"Do you think you can finish your audition?" I asked. "I'll
take care of the garbage can." I had never offered to clean up
anything gross like that ever before.

CHAD MORRIS & SHELLY BROWN

"I can't," McKell said. "Performing makes me sick. Like really, legit sick." She pulled the liner out of the can and held it tight. "The anxiety just takes over. I did the same thing during sixth-grade speeches—"

"Just try. They'll like you. I promise," I said. "And Danny . . ."

She looked up at me and I didn't finish my sentence. I was getting better at reading faces, even blurry faces. It wasn't the right time to push this.

McKell didn't believe she could do it.

And now she wouldn't finish Danny's challenge.

As she walked away with the garbage liner, McKell started bawling.

Part of me wanted to cry too. Not only had the worst thing happened, but I closed one eye and then the other before admitting to myself that there was a problem with my new eye.

CHAPTER 27

A CRYING BUSH

My grandpa taught me better than to let a lady carrying a bag of her own vomit just walk away. He didn't actually have a story for that one, but I was pretty sure that he would want me to help. I had no idea what to do. Did McKell want me with her? Would she rather be alone? A lot of the time *I* wanted to be alone, but McKell wasn't like me.

I could text her to see how she was doing, but that didn't seem like the right thing to do. I figured the least I could do was to follow her home at a distance and make sure she got there safely.

By the time I got outside, McKell had dropped the bag in the dumpster and was carrying her ukulele down the street.

She was a couple of blocks ahead so I hoped that she wouldn't think I was creepy following her.

When she got to the library she went around back. I knew where she was going. I slowed down. To give her some time. Quiet time to think and work things out in her head. Eventually, I reached the library and made my way through the parking lot to the wooded path. I could hear the birds chirping in the trees as I made my way up the path. It was beautiful. Even with my blurry eye I could see twice as much as I could the last time I was on this path. Rays of sunshine glittered in the air along the trail. There were so many shades of green, above me, in front of me, below my feet.

Maybe it was just a little problem with my eye. I really liked seeing and didn't want that to change.

I got across the stream much easier this time, hopping from rock to rock like McKell had done. I reached the other side dry.

Before I knew it, I climbed over a toppled trunk and was face to face with an eight-foot bush. A blurry bush.

An eight-foot, blurry, crying bush.

An eight-foot, blurry, crying, ukulele-playing bush.

I wasn't going in there. That just seemed too forceful. I backtracked to sit on the trunk and wait.

The ukulele playing stopped. McKell's head poked out of the hole and looked up at me.

I guess she'd heard me moving.

Her eyes were swollen and red. "Squint, you scared me. What are you doing here?"

"I . . . was worried," I said. I was using all of my self-control not to dive-bomb into a spiral of every word that was in my head. They all wanted to come out but she didn't need my blabber-mouthing.

"You can come in if you want." She backed herself into the bush.

I crawled in, trying to give her a lot of room once I was inside. Of course that was hard to do in such a small space. Inside, the bush never ceased to be magical. The green light, the small twisting, hanging branches. Even if it was fading in and out of blurriness.

McKell sniffled. "Your eye really doesn't look good."

Why did everyone have to say that? "I'm not here to talk about my eye."

"Why did you follow me?"

"Um," I stalled, trying to think of how to answer. "I wanted to make sure that you were okay." I let the silence hang there for a moment. "Are you?" I realized my question might not be clear. "Okay?"

More tears, her ukulele now on her lap. "I failed, Squint. And not just a little. Like this is a big fail. I failed you . . . I didn't follow through on our deal. I failed Danny—" She really choked up. "I couldn't do his last challenge. I knew this would happen. I just knew it. That's why I fought you so hard about doing the auditions. That's why I fought Danny too. I have terrible stage fright. My head goes wonky, like all of the blood slips down to my toes. I get an instant headache, my hearing goes muffled, my stomach gets sick. Every time. Every. Stupid. Time."

She picked her ukulele up and started strumming fast and angry. I had no idea that tiny instrument could sound so fierce. She slowed down, soft and sad. Soon it faded. "I'm failing," she said. "At everything. I'm failing at school. There's no way I can get as good of grades as my dad wants. I'm failing socially . . ." Was that last one my fault? "I'm failing at life. And my mom is no help. And my dad is trying to act like nothing's wrong. Like he didn't lose a son, and his wife isn't slowly going crazy, and his daughter isn't a total failure." She brought her knees up and rested her head against them.

"I don't think it's as bad as—" I started, wishing I could see her clearly.

"It is," she insisted, cutting me off.

"No," I said, "I—"

"It is," she repeated.

"No, it isn't. At least you *have* a mom and dad," I said, surprised at how it slipped out. But I didn't stop. "At least you had a brother. At least you weren't the kid born with the genetic disease. And at least you *have* a social life to fail at." I knew that she wasn't trying to make me upset, but the thoughts flowed through me like lightning through Squint's daggers.

McKell opened her mouth before saying anything. "I didn't mean . . ." We sat there not looking at each other.

Then without a word, she left.

I had screwed up.

I hadn't said the right things. I might have driven away my one and only almost-friend.

And my eye wasn't good enough to see her clearly as she went.

CHAPTER 28

REJECTION

I walked into my house and threw down my backpack.

That wasn't the way things were supposed to work out. McKell was supposed to show them her awesome rhyming and everyone was supposed to be completely wowed. She was supposed to realize that she was an amazing person with serious talent and be proud of herself. She was supposed to feel good about doing Danny's challenges and finally have a way to show how much she loved and appreciated him.

And then maybe she might even sit next to me again.

That was a whole string of "supposed tos" that hadn't happened. Not even close. And my eye wasn't *supposed to* be giving me problems again. Especially with my comic due tomorrow.

MIDDLE-SCHOOL RULE: If anything can go totally, completely, epically wrong, it will.

I kicked my backpack.

"I'm not sure what that backpack did to you, but you might need to kick it a few more times." Grandpa swiveled his orange recliner around to face me. "What's wrong?"

I turned away from him. "I don't really want to talk about it." I could only imagine he would have a football story for me. And that was about the last thing I wanted right now.

"Is something wrong with your friend?" Grandpa asked.

I shook my head. It was kind of a lie, but I did it.

"Is it your comic?" he asked.

"I don't care about my comic," I said, walking into the kitchen. And I didn't. Not now. Why had everything gone wrong? She had come so close to trying out, to doing the challenge. I sat at the kitchen table and let my head fall against the wood.

"Well," Grandma said, looking up from her old laptop. She had been typing at the counter. "What critter creeped in your basement?"

"I said I don't want to talk about it." Why did they both have to ask?

"Talk or don't talk, you've got to be careful," Grandma said. "You just slammed your head on that table and your eye's still fragile."

"No, it isn't," I said.

"Yes, sir," Grandma said. "Just because you're seeing clearly now, doesn't mean that—"

"I'm not seeing clearly," I blurted out. "It's going blurry again."

"What?" Grandma moved quickly across the kitchen, sat down next to me, and tilted my head back so she could look into my eye. "Oh, my goodness, look how red that is. What did you do, child?"

"Nothing," I said. "It just happened."

She let go of my face and called into the other room. "Keith, come look at this."

"What's going on?" Grandpa asked. "Is his backpack out for revenge?"

"No," Grandma said, "his eye. It's really red and he says it's blurry again."

Grandpa came over and looked so close his long beard brushed against my face. "Hmm, looks murky, too. It may be nothing. But it may be a problem. Let's call the doctor."

A few minutes later, we were traveling down to Dr. Young's office. They were staying open late for us.

The doctor looked at my eye with his instruments from all sorts of angles then said exactly what I didn't want to hear: "It looks like corneal rejection."

"That sounds bad," Grandma said.

He explained that my body's immune system thought that Danny's cornea wasn't a normal part of my body. It wasn't, but we wanted it to think it was so it would adopt the new windshield. But it was trying to get it to go away. Stupid body. I remembered that one of the videos I'd watched before my surgery had talked about corneal rejection. The dude went blind in that eye.

"It happens sometimes," the doctor said. "I'll give you some eye drops and hopefully that will take care of the problem."

"That's it?" Grandpa said. "Eye drops and it's fine?"

"Well," the doctor said, "in the majority of cases, drops are all it will take."

I didn't like those words, "In the majority." What if I wasn't in the majority?

"Everyone's different," the doctor explained. "We actually need to suppress the immune system to help your eye accept the new cornea. And it was good you rushed down. The sooner we start on the drops, the better."

"But what if my body won't accept the cornea?" I asked. "What if the drops aren't good enough?"

"Then it will lead to other complications," the doctor said. "But let's cross that bridge if we get there."

CHAPTER 29

THE FIGHT

We sipped hot cocoa around the table in the kitchen. I guess with the possibility of my eye going terrible, we could use something to cheer us up.

"Do you remember when we lost the last game of the season when you were a third grader?" Grandpa asked.

"No," I said. I wasn't in the mood for a story, but Grandpa was determined to tell it. At least this one had me in it.

"It was a huge disappointment," Grandpa said. "We should have won. We made a few bad plays and the refs didn't help us."

"Okay." I put a few more marshmallows in my cocoa. With the kind of day I'd had, I needed them.

"And the season was over. You." He pointed at me. "You were dead tired. You'd taken a few really hard hits."

"Okay." I sighed. I felt like I'd just taken a few hard hits again. My head was hurting, my heart was hurting, my eye was hurting, and I really didn't care about this memory right now.

"Do you remember what you wanted to do when we got home?" Grandpa asked.

I rested my elbows on the table and put my head in my hands. "Nope."

"You wanted to play catch," Grandpa said. "You wanted to do what you could to get better. You wanted to practice." He said the last line like it was the great moral to the story.

"I'm trying to get your point," I said.

Grandpa gave a tight-lipped grin. "I know this news is hard, but I think there's only one thing you can do."

"Lose my eyesight and quit playing?" I asked, thinking about what I'd done with football the next year.

"There was nothing you could do about your eyes," Grandpa said, wagging his finger. He pushed himself up from the table and went to the sink to wash his mug. "You would have kept playing if you could. But there *is* something you can do with your comic. Now."

"Grandpa's right," Grandma said. "I know you don't feel like it, but you have to finish that comic. It's due tomorrow."

My insides felt like they were going to explode like the planet Krypton had when it built up too much pressure in its uranium core. "I don't want to," I said. Nothing had worked right. And my comic wasn't good enough anyway.

"Flint, no more excuses," Grandma said. "I know it's hard, but—"

"No," I repeated. "It won't work anyway. I'm not going to win."

"That's not the right attitude," Grandma said.

"No." I shook my head.

"Why—" Grandpa started.

"No," I shook my head. "No, no, no—"

"Just tell us why?" Grandma asked, her eyebrows dipping.

"Because everything I try always fails," I said, thumping my fist against the table. I stood up. "I can't do anything. I can't play football without my eyes freaking out. I can't draw right. I can't keep friends. I can't even keep a new eye. Everything I try just—"

"Now, wait," Grandpa said. "Did you know that—"

"I don't care about football." I threw my hands in the air. "I can't play it. Every time I hear about it, it hurts."

"Now, listen—" Grandma said standing up and putting her hands on her hips.

"No," I said, the veins in my head beating against my skull. "I'm done. I'm not trying anymore." I looked at Grandma because she was pestering me the most. "Quit trying to make me."

"I'm only—" she started.

"Just quit," I said.

My vision was still a little blurry, but I could tell Grandma's eyes were open larger than I'd ever seen. She sniffled and her mouth moved, not really trying to talk. More like it didn't know what it wanted to do.

"I just want you to leave me alone," I told her.

And Grandma stormed out of the room.

Grandpa turned to me.

"Don't lecture me," I blurted out. I definitely wasn't in the mood. "It was you who—"

"Stop," Grandpa said, raising his palm.

"I—"

"Stop right there," he said, his voice stern. Extremely stern. Trying not to lose his cool. I'd heard him use that voice before. He gritted his teeth like he was about to go after a ref who'd made a terrible call, and he pointed at my chair. "Sit down and listen."

I never wanted to be one of those refs.

I sat.

"Listen carefully," Grandpa said, his voice still filled with intensity. "You need to know something."

"I don't want to finish—" I said, gathering my wits again. I didn't want to be pushed into anything.

"I said *listen*," Grandpa said, his voice rising.

"I'm not the one who—" I said.

"Your grandmother hasn't eaten lunch in months," he said, cutting me off.

"And how's that supposed to—" I started, then what he'd said sank in. "What?"

"Your grandmother hasn't eaten lunch in months," he

repeated slowly and deliberately. "Do you remember how she loved going out to eat with her friends?" I nodded. He stood up and started pacing the room. "Well, she used to go every Tuesday and Thursday with those ladies from work. It was her favorite thing. But I noticed months ago that she had missed a few times. She told me she was just trying to save a little money." He looked at me for a moment, almost daring me to interrupt. "Then after a few more times," he continued, "she used the excuse that she was tired of doing the same thing. Then I noticed that she was spending more time online. Just yesterday I found out that she's got a second job, typing out doctors' notes. They send her pictures of the notes and she types them in to some computer program when I'm on the night shift or I'm watching TV."

"Okay," I said, still trying to figure out what this had to do with me.

"She fixes all of our clothes by hand," Grandpa added.

"I know," I said.

"Not your clothes. You get new clothes. She fixes her clothes and sometimes my clothes," he said. "She uses coupons at the grocery store. She uses a box kit to dye her hair. She hasn't seen her hairstylist in I don't know how long. She saves change that she finds in the machines at work. But it was only when I noticed that she wasn't eating lunch at all that I called her on it."

"So?" I asked.

"She does all of that for you," Grandpa said. "To save

money. For that eye of yours. Both of them, really. And she knows we don't have the money to help you in all the ways other people could. She went without her favorite thing for months. She's been sacrificing. She's been working."

"I didn't—"

"We still don't know how we're going to pay for the rest of your surgery," he interrupted, his hands in the air. "But she's trying. I'm trying." His voice was excited again.

I had no idea. I mean, I knew she didn't make sandwiches with me. I hadn't heard about her visits with her friends for a while. And I knew she spent a lot of time on the computer. I just didn't know why. And I hadn't stopped to think about how we were going to pay for the surgery . . . or the new clothes I had to get because of the surgery . . . or the new ink pens we picked up last month when my old ones ran dry . . . I just . . .

"And she thought that maybe if you could submit something to the contest . . . " Grandpa said, waving his arms again. "I mean, you talked about nothing else for months. And if you won something, then maybe you would forgive us, and . . ." He stopped to swallow. "And it might help you to be happy."

"Forgive you?" I asked.

"For not being your real parents," he said. "For being old and poor, and not being able to give you everything."

I stared at him.

"She's terrified of losing you like we lost your mom," he said. He turned away and slowly walked to the sink. He leaned against it, folded his arms, and looked at the ceiling. I didn't know all of the story between my grandparents and my mom. I knew my mom and Grandma had fought a lot. And I knew my mom ran away from home when she was a teenager and had made some terrible decisions with a lot of bad consequences. A lot. Like she couldn't take care of me anymore. But I never once thought that Grandma would be scared of the same thing happening to me.

When I really let it all sink in, I realized that I hadn't thought much about Grandma at all. She was like a side character in a comic that didn't have a well-thought-out backstory. And I'd never tried to learn it.

"Your grandmother can be a brash woman," Grandpa said. "She says what she thinks. But she loves you." He looked right at me. "She loves you," he repeated. He let out a huge sigh and stood. "I do too. We aren't young. We know we can't give you what others give their kids. But we do love you."

And then Grandpa turned and left me alone in the kitchen.

CHAPTER 30

MORE THAN I DID

I lay in my bed for a long time. I hadn't seen it. I had no idea. I had a new eye and I had started to see everything differently. I saw the flaws in my art. I saw a girl who needed a friend. I'd started to be able to read people's faces a little. I saw a boy for the amazing way he made those around him better, in spite of his disability. But I hadn't seen my own grandparents working so hard for me.

I hadn't seen it.

I ate every day. Never really suffered. All the while my grandma was skipping lunch to try to save money for me. For my new eye.

My own grandma.

And I treated her like a side character.

It must have broken her heart when I wouldn't draw after all she sacrificed.

I rolled over.

What else wasn't I seeing?

Like McKell couldn't see that having a mom in pajamas was just fine. Like I was embarrassed about my grandparents all of the time, but I didn't need to be.

Mom.

My mom was another story. Grandma and Grandpa tried so hard to help me, but my mom hadn't done hardly anything. When she actually visited, it was okay, it was nice enough. But it had been months. Months. A lot of texted promises, but she hadn't come through.

I had completely stopped answering her texts. She didn't deserve it.

Unless there was something else I hadn't seen.

I tried really hard to think about my mom and what I was missing. There was a saying in comics that every character, big or small, is the hero in their own story—even the villains. Commissioner Gordon puts his life on the line for the citizens of Gotham City. Magneto wants the best for the mutants. What would the story look like if my mom was the hero?

I didn't know.

But Grandma. She really was a hero, and I hadn't seen it. Completely missed it. Something inside me was glad that she wanted me to draw, to try. I hated it, but I loved it too. She somehow thought that I might win something. That I was good enough. She believed in me more than I did.

So did Grandpa.

They believed in me more than I believed in myself.

More.

And I needed that.

McKell was the same way. I thought of her insisting that I draw. I thought of her reaction when she'd read my comic. She believed in me too.

Danny was that same way for McKell. He thought her songs were fantastic.

I was that way for McKell. But she couldn't see it. She was the one with vision problems there. She couldn't see her own talent, how seriously cool she was just being herself. Danny and I could see it, but she couldn't.

I still felt terrible that her audition had gone so bad. She was so talented. And she tried so hard. Just being in that room and getting up on the stage was more than she'd ever done before. But she was so nervous, so anxious, she couldn't do it.

I wished there was a way I could . . .

All of a sudden, I had an idea.

Maybe everyone needed someone who believed in them more than they did. I couldn't wait to talk to McKell.

But first, I moved over to my desk and pulled out a page. I clenched my eyes shut for a moment.

No one expected a thirteen-year-old to win this contest. I didn't expect it anymore either. And maybe I wouldn't shatter anyone's expectations, but I could at least finish what I'd started.

CHAPTER 31

INVINCIBLE

"I'm not going to try out again," McKell said. "Even if I wanted to, the auditions are over." Thankfully, she had agreed to meet me at the plant cave after school.

I reached into my portfolio case and handed her some pages. "I scanned it and sent it in this morning," I said. I'd hardly slept the night before getting it done.

"You did? Even with your eye problems?" I had told her about the corneal rejection and the drops. Grandma said my eye was looking better, but I wasn't sure. It was still really irritated.

I nodded. She looked up at me then down at the papers.

"It's not good enough," I said, "but I finished."

She knew what I was doing, trying to persuade her, but she looked at them anyway.

Squint stepped out into the open. Alone.

He knew what he was going to face. He knew his chances were next to nothing, but he had to try.

He had spent all night tracking down Gunn and the others. They hadn't stayed in the metallic castle. That place had been compromised. Thankfully Diamond had a few hints as to where they might have gone.

And he found them here, on a small island in the Northern Sea. Waves dashed against the bottom of the cliffs, but the top rose to a fairly barren plateau the size of a small town. A building chiseled into the cliffside must be where they were keeping the Empress.

But Squint wasn't going in. He had a plan.

"Centurions," Squint screamed, "wherever you go, I will find you!" He pulled out his daggers and sliced the edges of the cliffs into the water below. "Come and face me."

And then he waited in the center of the plateau, the waves crashing so high they nearly met the cliff tops.

Until . . .

Four people floated above him, riding on their capes: blue, yellow, green, and white. Gunn, the large boy with the blue cape, landed first on one corner of the plateau. "You shouldn't have come here, Squint," he yelled over the waves. "You couldn't handle two of us, what makes you think you'll be able to handle all four?" He raised his fire bazooka.

Traz leapt off his green cape and punched a boulder into the ground. "I like the patch," Traz said. "Were you hoping we would take out the other eye too?"

Lash, with her yellow cape and red hair, glided to the ground. She pulled out her laser whips, slinging them over her head in wide arcs and curls. "Sorry I missed you last time, Squint. I won't miss you today." She whipped a branch off a nearby tree with surprising accuracy.

And Madame Cool leapt off her white cape, landing nimbly on the ground in the other corner. "I hope you weren't looking for a warm welcome." She unsheathed two long blades of ice and swung them, a barrage of icicles shooting out at Squint.

Squint dove to the ground, letting the attack pass over him. He couldn't see it yet, but he had a theory that both Lash and Madame Cool would have dark scales growing on the backs of their necks as well. Squint had found an old scroll that mentioned an ancient magic that brought darkness into people. And scales showed the darkness's growth. Not only were these trained supernatural soldiers, but likely supernatural soldiers heightened by darkness.

"Where's your cape?" Gunn asked. "Or did you not care about being bulletproof when you came?" He fired, Squint leaping to the side.

"I must have forgotten it," Squint said, flipping back onto his feet. He moved his head from side to side, trying to make sure no one could get too far to his right where he couldn't see.

They were all there. Gunn with his fireball bazooka, Traz with his boulder gloves, Lash with her laser whips, and Madame Cool with her icy blasts.

COMIC RULE: Endings have to be epic.

With a synchronized attack, Squint's old friends blasted at him. He shot with his light-daggers, jumped, and weaved, trying to stay alive. He curled over a fireball and ducked under icicles while slicing a boulder in half.

COMIC RULE: Comic-book heroes can do things that would be impossible to do in real life. But we all love them and want them to, so it's fine.

"Give up, Squint," Gunn shouted, ready to fire again. "You don't belong with us."

Squint didn't answer.

"Watch out for his dog," Traz said. "Unless we lucked out and he's dead, he'll be around here somewhere."

A swish of red and Traz was hurled to the side. "I think you should look out for more than his dog."

It was Diamond, flying in on Squint's cape.

Squint smiled. It felt so good not to be alone.

Diamond's attack split the group.

Gunn and Madame Cool turned on her while Lash and a recovering Traz went after Squint. Thankfully his cape came to him. Diamond already had her impenetrable casing.

More blazes and shouts.

"Just hold out," Squint told himself. "For the plan to work, we just have to hold out."

But eventually the other Centurions were too much. When dodging a whip, Traz caught Squint with a boulder again. Before he could recover, Lash stole a dagger with her whip. Squint saw the scales on her neck, but knowing his theory might be confirmed couldn't help him now.

Diamond fought hard, but eventually took a blast of icicles on the left side of her body, and when a fireball hit her, the unthinkable happened.

CRACK!

Her hard diamond exterior fractured and a huge section of it fell to the ground. There she was, her light brown face exposed and nearly half of her body in a white suit, no longer protected. She wasn't as invincible as she thought.

"With enough force," Gunn said, "even diamonds can be broken." He raised his fire bazooka.

Squint raced to save Diamond, but took a boulder to the back, sending his last dagger flying. Another boulder pinned his cape to the ground.

No bulletproof cape. No daggers. Four enemies. And a friend in terrible danger.

"Aaahh!" Squint took a whip across his side and back.

Gunn leveled his bazooka at the half-broken Diamond.

"Noooooo!" Squint screamed.

And then everything changed.

Light blasted from beneath Squint's eyepatch, a huge thick stream of it. The light pummeled Gunn, throttling him to near the edge of the cliff.

"What was that?" Traz asked, whirling around.

Squint didn't know, but he didn't stop to ask questions. He screamed again, but this time light blasted out of both his eyes and slammed into Traz.

What was happening?

All of the Centurions focused on him. But the light wouldn't stop. Squint felt it run down his arms, and he shot it out his fingers. Then again out his other hand. Light was pouring out of him in powerful streams. Each time one of the Centurions tried to mount a counterattack, Squint pummeled them with light.

It was four on one, but the one was winning.

Until Traz took another shot, letting Lash sneak up on Squint from behind.

She whipped around his neck.

But then Lash went down.

Squint turned to see Diamond, still fighting even without all of her diamond shield.

"I guess you don't need a shield to be invincible," Squint said.

Diamond smiled. "You're glowing," she said.

And Squint was. His eyes were a brilliant white and his limbs nearly burned with light. "I don't know how," he said. "It's like it's in me."

A howl.

That was their signal.

Their plan had worked. While they were fighting, Rock had found the Empress and brought her to a hidden crevasse in the rock, where she could wait until they could safely take her from the island.

McKell flipped over the last page. "Amazing," she said. "I mean, there was a ton of fighting, which I guess you need in comic books, but you did great work."

"Thanks," I said. It almost felt magical. McKell reading my comic inside the plant cave.

"Seriously good work," she said, nodding. I cursed my stupid eye that blurred my vision and didn't let me see clearly how excited she really was. "I don't know what kind of competition you're up against for the contest, but you've got to have a good chance."

I'm sure I smiled huge.

"I liked all the light Squint shot out," she said.

"I do too," I said. "What about Diamond? What did you think of her?"

"I guess she's invincible," she said. "More than even she thought."

"Definitely," I said.

She shifted on the ground and carefully set my comic sheets on top of my portfolio. "You know it's not us versus them," she said. "Right?"

I looked at her for a while. "Maybe," I said.

"And that I'm not Diamond," she said. "I'm no hero." She picked up a branch off the ground.

"I know," I said. "She's just made up. You're better."

"No, I'm not," she said, drawing on the ground with the stick. "I couldn't even finish—"

"Look," I said. "I'm not Squint either. But it—"

"I didn't do anything in real life," she said. "I couldn't even finish Danny's challenges." She dug the branch into the ground.

"You did a lot of them," I said.

"What?" she asked.

"You tried," I said.

"That's not good enough," she said, dropping her stick. "I didn't try his challenges until it was too late. I didn't even sing in the audition."

"Okay," I said. "But you did . . ." I tried to think of how to say it. I couldn't think of the words. Rambling crazy me couldn't think of what to say. "Did you notice that in my story, Diamond always seems to be doing the same thing?"

"What?" McKell said. "Punching people with her awesome diamond hands?" She mimicked a punch.

"No," I said. "Well, yes, but she's always . . ." I trailed off for a second, something caught in my throat. "She's always," I started over again, "saving Squint."

I was quiet for a moment, hoping that would sink in.

"Maybe you didn't do everything you hoped for," I said. "But you did eat lunch with a lonely kid. And—" I couldn't help it. Tears welled up in my eyes. "And—"

"Squint—" she started.

"No," I said. "Let me say this. I just . . . I don't know how. You know I ramble, but you were super brave and showed me you. And *you're* really cool. You should be proud of you. I like you. And because of you I have a friend for the first time in a very long time. And I started to care for the first time in a long time. And . . . I don't know how to say this kind of stuff."

"You don't have to," she said. "I just—"

"I need to get this out. I just think you're on the right trail. You won me over. You keep doing this, just being you and reaching out to people like you did to me and . . ."

My blurry eye didn't let me completely see her, and the tears didn't help either. But it kind of helped me speak my mind.

"Stop," McKell said.

"No," I said. "I have one more thing to say. I'm not Danny. I'm not even close. But I'm proud of you." I took a deep breath. "And I can only imagine Danny is too."

CHAD MORRIS & SHELLY BROWN

She looked at me and tears welled up in her eyes too. "But I didn't finish," she said.

"All I know is that I have a friend for the first time in a very long time," I said. "And I'm pretty sure that's your fault." I swallowed. "Thanks."

"Thanks for being my friend back," she said. "Sorry that I didn't always hang out with—"

"No worries," I said. "And . . . if you want to try to finish the challenges, I have an idea."

"I already tried," she said.

"No," I said. "What if I thought of a way that you could show everyone your awesome rhyming, your ukulele playing, but you don't have to go on a stage?"

Her face softened. "I don't know what you're even saying, but I don't know if I'm willing to risk it."

"What if I risk it with you?" I said. "You're the only one I've ever shown my drawings to. Well, except my grandma and grandpa. And Gavin and the others saw them and made fun of them pretty good. So I'm kind of terrified of anyone else seeing them."

I told her my idea. I didn't present it very well—I rambled more than I should have, but she didn't seem to hate it.

"That's a lot of work for a kid who should be resting his eyes," McKell said.

"It'd be worth it."

She looked at my red eye for a moment. One friend looking at another friend in a plant cave where they had laughed and cried together. "If we do this," she finally said, "I think I'd want to put together a different song."

"So . . . you'll try?" I asked.

"I said, *if*," she said.

"And?" I asked.

"Maybe," she said.

"Look," I said. "My eye might be going, but I'd really love to see you do this."

CHAPTER 32

A FAVOR

I was supposed to be in the auditorium with McKell. I told her I'd meet her there. A week had passed since I pitched my idea, and it turned out to be barely enough time. I hoped people would like it.

But I was sweating for a different reason.

I felt like Squint, basically picking a fight with the four other Centurions. But this time I didn't have Rock sneaking in, and I didn't have Diamond watching my back. I was completely alone.

I looked over at Gavin, Travis, Chloe, and Emma walking together toward the assembly. I took a deep breath.

With every step closer to them, I felt less and less like a hero.

Could I really do this? But I thought of what was on the line. "Hey," I said.

No one stopped.

"Hey, Gavin," I said louder and tapped him on the shoulder.

Gavin looked over, then did a double take when he saw who it was. "Hey, Squint." He wrinkled his brow.

"I miss the patch," Travis said. "Dread Pirate Four-Eyes," he said in his pirate voice. "Can you bring it back? I had so much more material."

"Sorry," I said. "My eyes are doing okay." And thankfully they were. Over the last week, the drops seemed to be doing their job. It was still a little early to tell, but the doctor was optimistic. Of course, my left eye still had its problems, but it wasn't nearly as bad as my right eye had been.

Chloe and Emma watched silently.

"Gavin, can I talk to you for a minute?" I asked.

I had a theory. McKell had been so different when she wasn't with everyone else. Maybe that was true with other people too. Maybe that was a middle-school rule. Maybe when people didn't feel like they had to look cool for everyone else, they might be a little different. Maybe I could talk to the Gavin who used to share his Doritos with me at lunch and would invite me over for pick-up games. The Gavin who ran and got the coach when I sprained my ankle in peewee football. He had to be in there too. But I could totally get the Gavin who called me names in the halls and made fun of my comics instead.

"Why?" Gavin said.

I knew it wouldn't be easy. I just hoped he didn't pull out a fireball bazooka and blast me into oblivion. "Please?" I asked. "Just for a second."

He looked at his friends. Travis shrugged. Emma and Chloe started talking to each other, probably about how strange I was.

"I guess," Gavin said, in a tone that made it clear that he was humoring a crazy kid. He slowed and we walked a little behind the group.

I had thought so much about this, coming up with countless versions of our dialogue, but I still felt completely unprepared. Just about every way I could say this could blow up in my face. Or it just wouldn't work.

"I have a favor to ask."

"I have a favor to ask you," Gavin said. "Quit asking for favors." He laughed to himself, but with his other friends watching from a distance, they didn't hear the joke and his laugh died out quickly. Maybe getting him away from them had worked a little.

"I need you to talk to the others for me." I kept going. "McKell is going to do something really brave today. And not that she needs your approval or anything, but if you didn't make fun of her I think that would be . . ." It sounded stupid coming out of my mouth.

"Like in the talent show?" Gavin asked.

"Yeah," I said. "Just don't—"

"I got it," he said.

"I mean it, though."

"I heard you," Gavin said and started to walk back.

"Wait," I said. "Are you going to—"

"I don't know," Gavin said. "I'll watch it. Maybe I'll tease her a little if it's stupid, but I tease everyone. It's not a big deal. Besides, she's been ditching us to sit with you."

That was true. Every day for the last week. I hadn't sat alone.

Every day.

"Sometimes teasing might be a big deal," I said. "I mean, she's had the talent the whole time she's been here, but was afraid to show you."

Gavin looked at me for a moment then shook his head. "Why do you always look at me like I'm some sort of jerk?"

I wasn't expecting that. "Um . . ." How honest should I be here? Was this another setup? If I wanted his help, what should I say? For some reason, I decided to tell him the truth. "Because you make mean jokes about me. Because you make fun of my comics. You make me feel like I'm an idiot for having eye problems and wearing an eye patch. You called my house a shack."

"C'mon," Gavin said, interrupting. "I'm just messing around. Learn to take a joke."

Did he really think he was just joking around? That I was the one with the problem? Could he really not see how big of a jerk he was?

"This is what I'm talking about, Gavin," I said. "Sometimes the things you and your friends say to me . . ." I tried to find the words. "They . . . haunt me. Like I can't stop thinking about them. Like I wonder if there is a reason why no one's ever called me cute before. Or if my comics really are stupid. Or if . . . well, even more than that."

He stared for a moment. "But you used to be different," he said. "You used to tease back. We used to hang out. You used to be fun. Then you stopped."

Wait. Was he blaming me for our friendship ending? That I ditched him?

"But I'm not mean," I said.

"Sometimes silence is mean," he said. "Ignoring me is mean." He spat out the words. He had some feelings behind this.

Maybe I had somehow hurt him. I hadn't seen that coming. There was no way I would have thought that just trying to stay out of Gavin's way would bother him. In fact, I didn't think anything bothered him.

"I . . ." What should I say? "Just know that what you say can hurt people," I said. "And McKell is nervous. Try not to hurt her. Or, I guess, even if you joke, make sure it's clear that you're on her side." I swallowed. "If you are."

"She's kind of ditched us," Gavin said. "Like you."

And then he walked away.

That definitely wasn't how I hoped this would go.

CHAPTER 33

TALENT ASSEMBLY

I sat in the auditorium next to McKell. It was the day she had hoped to be able to be backstage, warming up on her ukulele. About to sing one of her own songs. About to make her brother proud. But she was going to be sitting in the audience with me. She hadn't even brought her uke. But we were both nervous.

Super nervous.

We sat in the back corner. If it didn't go well, we could make a quick getaway.

"Thanks for all your work," she said. "And for your idea."

I smiled. "No problem."

"Danny would have liked you," she said.

I shrugged. "Danny liked everyone."

"True," she said. "But he would have really liked you."

I couldn't stop thinking about my talk with Gavin. He really couldn't see how mean he was. Was I the same? Was I blind to ways I was mean? I was going to have to think about that. I still hoped he wouldn't make fun of McKell. I could take the teasing. I was kind of used to it. But I didn't want him messing with McKell.

We sat through the first acts. Caleb did his yo-yo. JanaLee did her peaceful piano thing. There was a rock band that was a bit too loud to understand, and a bunch of boys came out and flexed and sort of danced to some pretty fast music. I'm not really sure what their talent was, but they had a lot of energy. After each act, I think my heart rate doubled. We were getting closer. It was almost our time.

I had no idea how it would go over. I imagined Gavin laughing and yelling out, "What is this?"

Travis would say something like, "How did this even get into the show?"

Chloe would ask, "Did anyone ever tell them that they were talented before?"

And Emma would roll her eyes.

I shook my head. At this point, it was happening.

Both of the student announcers came out on the stage again. The boy, Jared, I think, tried to crack a joke about all the energy the last act had. He didn't really say it right and it didn't get many laughs. He smiled anyway.

"This next act," the girl announcer, Hillary, said, "is a song that was written by someone at our school."

This was it.

McKell clutched at my arm like we were about to go over the first hill of a roller-coaster.

"Ouch," I said, her fingers digging into my arm.

"Sorry," she said, and let up, but still wouldn't let go.

The curtain opened and the large screen slowly started to descend.

"Yep," Jared said into his microphone. "McKell Panganiban wrote and will perform her own song." I think he pronounced every vowel wrong in her last name. Totally butchered it. But McKell didn't seem to care.

"With a little help from some art by Flint Minett," Hillary added. It felt so weird to hear my name over the speaker system, especially my real name.

More thoughts of what Gavin and the others could be saying filled my brain.

"And some video editing by a guy named Yellow," Jared said. He looked offstage. "Is that the right name?" He wasn't speaking in the microphone, but I could still hear his question. "Yes," he said. "That is his name. The song is called 'Invincible.'"

The audience gave the same half-hearted applause they gave to most acts before they started.

The video flashed on and focused on McKell's hand strumming a ukulele. Beside it, hand-drawn musical notes came out and floated across the screen. Thanks to Yellow, we had combined McKell's music with my drawing. And thankfully, Mrs. Lin and Mr. Mueller were kind enough to let us enter the video in late. I'm sure Mrs. Lin was extra lenient because of how sick McKell had been when she auditioned.

McKell's smooth voice echoed over the sound system.

> *If I was covered, almost smothered in steel, I'd be*
> *real . . . invincible.*

A picture of a girl covered in steel crossed the screen. I'd made her look kind of like a female Colossus.

> *No one could attack, and crack how I feel, real*
> *invincible.*

With each beat, either a picture or a written word flashed. I focused on the word *invincible* this time. All the drawings had taken a decent amount of time, but Yellow made them flash in perfect time. I know he had to work really hard to make it happen.

Now the video backed out to show McKell. She sat on a stool in her room, wearing some makeup. It was simple, nothing like Grandma's. And her hair was curled a little. She looked great. And her voice sounded fantastic. Like something you would hear on the radio.

> *Hard like a diamond and strong like a lion,*
> *invincible.*

My pictures of Diamond flashed across the screen. I still really liked that character. Of course a lion followed. That had taken some time.

Just be me, never care what others think. Invincible.

McKell changed rhythms, longer, and slower. The strumming calmed. The video focused on McKell's face. No drawings for this part.

Maybe we all want to be—

She drew out that last word and her strumming built louder.

Then a burst of words, all rattled out in speed, but said so clearly—

> *But sometimes I fall, mess up it all, feel broken,*
> *unspoken, how I'm dying inside, say I'm fine,*
> *but I'm lyin', so scared, and unprepared. Can't*
> *be me, they'll all see, that I'm just not—*

The strumming calmed.

Invincible.

She repeated the word in a kind of soft but catchy chorus.

I looked around. Everyone in the auditorium sat quietly watching. I don't think they expected the song to be this good. The video to be this good.

McKell loosened her grip on my arm. She must have realized that we weren't bombing. Not even close.

Her voice came in again and she tightened her grip. If she was this nervous watching herself, I was glad I hadn't pushed her too far to perform in public.

> *Maybe it's time, draw a line, redefine what it means,*
> *   invincible.*
> *After you stumble, or crumble and fall, you stand*
> *   tall, that's invincible.*
> *Try and try, and not hide it inside, so invincible.*
> *Show who you are, your beauty, your scars, that's*
> *   invincible.*

She did the same chorus again, louder and strong this time. Then my favorite part. Danny always challenged McKell to make sure that she included herself in her songs, her personality, her uniqueness. And I thought this was it.

The camera closed in on the uke as she banged it twice. She strummed sharp while blurting out rhymes faster than I'd ever seen her do before. Almost like rapping, but with a melody.

> *And I smile a while, this trial compiles, compounds*
> *   around, but I rebound, this thing will never*
> *   keep me down. Never keep me down.*
> *I share my heart, and start to shine, stand up for me,*
> *   and see this time, make a friend, again, and*
> *   hope it will never end. Never end.*
> *I watch a comedy, to remedy some blues, I choose to*

face a fear and with tears conquer through to
cheers. I'm so glad to be right here.
I look up, look out, speak up, speak out, I can sing,
and bring, this voice of choice to everyone who'll
listen to my sound. I won't be kept down.

She sounded so strong. So good.

I won't be kept down.

And I heard it off to my side as well. The real McKell was singing along.

One more chorus of the word *invincible.*

"I can't just sit here," McKell said, and got up to walk out of the auditorium. The song was ending and it was getting too much for her. Even though people seemed to like it, she was going to be sick again.

The video faded as applause started. It grew louder and louder.

I looked over to see McKell stopped in the doorway.

The applause kept going. Like they really liked it. A few people whistled. It went on for a long time. That doesn't happen very often with a junior high crowd.

I joined in.

And no one clapped louder or longer than me.

CHAPTER 34

SPAGHETTI AND A LETTER

I stood over the boiling pasta waiting for it to be done. Spaghetti isn't that hard to make, but I was still hoping I wouldn't mess it up.

Everything was going perfect until Grandma walked in. She took one step into the kitchen and froze.

"What are you doing in here?" I asked.

"Do I need a reason to walk into my own kitchen?" she asked back. "Are you *cooking*?"

"Grandpa," I yelled. "You were supposed to keep her out of here."

He came in shrugging. "She doesn't listen to me. You know that."

"You had one job," I said to Grandpa.

His beard bobbed as he chuckled.

I turned to Grandma who was still looking confused. "I'm making lunch for us." The water boiled over as if on cue. I gave a weak, "Surprise!" before turning down the stovetop and blowing on the foam coming over the pot.

"Well ain't you sweeter than molasses on sugarcane." Grandma gave me a hug from behind.

"I figured I owed you," I said, and tried to hug her back, but it was awkward with her still behind me.

"And don't claim he's sweet until after you've eaten it," Grandpa said standing in the doorframe. "I don't know about thirteen-year-olds cookin'."

GRANDMA AND GRANDPA RULE: If you're lucky enough to have a grandpa and grandma you should probably love them. And probably do your chores every now and again. Not all the time. You don't want to be perfect. And maybe you could even make them lunch. They might deserve it.

GRANDMA AND GRANDPA RULE: Listening to football stories is still optional.

After lunch I took off. Grandma had given me permission to cut a small bouquet of her spring flowers and I put them all in a bunch and tied them.

I jumped on my bike but by the time I reached McKell's house I was a windswept mess. Good ol' Nebraska wind almost knocked me off my bike a few times and the flowers were a little sadder than when I left.

My eye was healing up. It wasn't perfect, but the drops were going to do their job. Unless something unexpected happened, my body was going to accept the cornea after all.

Cars were lined up along the street just like before. Inside there were piles of shoes just like before.

McKell took my flowers and led me into the main room, where the picture of Danny was sitting on a low table surrounded by family members on folding chairs, dining room chairs, and couches. The photo had more candles around it now, a plate of food, Danny's Huskers hat, and some flowers. McKell put my flowers in water and put them with the others by the picture.

"First prayers, then a song, then balloons, then food," McKell said, prepping me for the evening's events. "You don't have to say the prayers if you don't want to. You don't have to do any of it if you don't want to. But thank you for coming."

"Thanks for inviting me," I said. McKell sat in the front with her parents, and I found myself a place in the back, allowing family to fill the closer seats. I had never heard anyone say prayers the way that they did. One person would speak and the others would respond in the same way—many times. I closed my eyes and listened to the almost-music of the repetition and smelled the candles and felt the warmth of so many bodies gathered to say farewell.

McKell called this celebration "Fortieth-Day Prayer."

Forty days after his death. The day that Danny's spirit went to heaven. It was a tradition from her father's Filipino side of the family.

After prayer a few family members got up to sing. Some songs were in English and some were not. The whole thing took a long time but it was nice, so I just listened. Her father then explained that they had balloons that they wanted to release. Everyone got up and went to the backyard. They had a large patio and even larger yard so people got their balloons and spread out.

McKell brought me a big white balloon. Her eyes were red and puffy but her smile seemed sincere. "So in my family, we find a quiet place and say a few words to the one who passed away, then release the balloon with the idea that the balloon will carry our message to heaven. I know that you don't know Danny that well but I figured you should get a balloon too." She handed me the string and walked away to get her balloon and find her quiet place.

I looked at the balloon as the wind whipped it around a bit. Say something to Danny, huh?

"Danny Panganiban," I started, and I was pretty proud that I could say his last name. "I know you don't really know me. I'm Flint but you can call me Squint if you want." I looked around to make sure that I wasn't the only person talking to a balloon. I wasn't.

"I wanted to tell you thanks. Because of you and your challenges, I met your sister. You'd be proud of her. Because of you she is braver . . . and happier. And I have a friend. And I really needed a . . ." I stopped. He could figure the rest out.

"And because of your YouTube channel I saw that a person could be different, look different, have struggles, make mistakes, and still have so much to offer." I sniffled. My darn nose was running. "I want to be like you."

I stood there for a minute. "Oh, and that whole eye business." I took a deep breath. "I got a letter yesterday. It's from the family of the person that gave me my eye." I paused. "Turns out it wasn't you." I gave a sad laugh. "I really, *really* wanted it to be you. It was some guy on the other side of town who liked hockey and horses. Yeah, not really you at all," I said.

"But I still wanted to say that even though I don't have your eye, in a lot of ways you still helped me to see." I stood there for a moment longer. "Really see."

The wind stopped. Everything was still and quiet.

I opened my hand and let the balloon float up into the sky.

CHAPTER 35

THE FINAL CHALLENGE

There was enough food set out to feed a small country. McKell introduced me to her *tito* and *tita*, and while we were talking, her dad got everyone's attention.

"Yellow just called," Danny's dad said. He took a second to explain who Yellow was for any family members who didn't know. "He told me that he is about to post Danny's last video, but he sent it to me so we can see it first."

Her dad synced his phone to the television in the family room. The screen was plenty big for all of us, and we all pulled up a seat or sat around the floor.

McKell's mom gave a small gasp when Danny's face appeared on the screen for the last time.

"Hello again," Danny said with a little less of his usual Danny-energy than in his other videos.

"This is my last video." He gave a tired smile. "Aww, I know . . . I'm sad too."

He went back to his cheerful voice but it was a little slower than before. "But if it's my last one then I'm going to make it count. You see, I have put my whole heart into this channel and I don't want to see it die." His smile dropped and he looked off camera. "Wait, I'm dying of heart disease, should I take that last part out?" You could see his eyes searching his own mind for an answer. "Nah, life is just ironic that way sometimes." He went back to smiling at the camera. "Enjoy a bite of irony on me. Mmmm—tastes like iron." He rubbed his belly then laughed.

He looked off camera again. "I told you I wasn't going to get through a video without joking around. I don't think I know how. Oh well, back to being serious." He said that last part like a news reporter would say, "This just in!"

Then he took a deep breath and did just as he said he would. He got serious. "I have made so many friends through this channel. The emails that I have received from you let me know that you've made a lot of friends too. And it hurts me a little to see this channel die with me. That's why I have asked Yellow to help me with something. And I'm going to ask you to help me as well."

I leaned in. I'd do it. Anything.

"Help me keep 'Danny's Challenges' alive. Post your own

challenges and tag them with the hashtag #DannysChallenges. Yellow will search the internet every other week for some of the best challenges and then post them here for others to see and follow."

McKell's dad gave a small whoop and clapped his hands a couple of times.

"So hit me with your best challenge for spreading kindness. A challenge that promotes gratitude. A challenge that creates joy for life. A challenge that helps people relate to people. They don't have to be complicated. Mine never were. Share a little piece of yourself, like I did, and let us get to know and love you."

He was right. Sharing little parts of himself made people love him. Even people like me, who never even met him.

Maybe I could do that.

Danny's smile got extra big. "Because that's what we're doing, spreading the love.

"And on that note I just wanted to leave one last message.

"I love you.

"I love you, Mom. I love you, Papa.

"I love you, McKell.

"I love you, family.

"I love you, my friends.

"I really do."

CHAPTER 36

A NEW COMIC

The Empress stood not much taller than Squint. She was only a few years older and wore a long silver dress. Her hair was long and silver too, nearly reaching the hard rocky ground of the island cliffs. She looked at Squint. "I see that you found out about me."

"What do you mean?" Squint asked. He had pulled off his cape and was looking to see how he might load everyone on. The magic flying cape was their only way from the island. They might not all fit. He may have to send them off the island two at a time. Hopefully they would escape before Gunn and the others woke up. He hoped they were knocked out for a while.

"I do have magic," the Empress said. "Powerful magic. But I didn't give you everything."

Squint looked at his hands; they were still glowing.

"The daggers," she said. "They were just tools, the light was always there. I simply gave you a way to let a little out. I chose you as a Centurion because of your light." She motioned where his patch had been. "It first came out where you had been weak. At times, it is our weaknesses that can make us better, let our light out."

Squint felt where his eye had been injured.

She turned to Diamond. "It is similar with you. If you focus, you can fill the hole in your diamond shield."

Rock barked. "And was the magic always inside of me?"

The Empress looked down, several strands of her silver hair falling over her large eyes. "No," she said. "You're just a bunch of rocks without me."

He barked again. "A little disappointing, but I can deal with it."

Squint looked back again to where they'd had their great battle and thought he saw some of his enemies stirring. "Let's get you out of here," he said to the Empress. "I'll send you across with Diamond, then send the cape back for me. That's assuming you don't want to just make another."

"No," the Empress said.

"Okay," Squint said. "Mine will have to do."

"No," the Empress repeated. "I'm not leaving."

Both Diamond and Squint looked back in disbelief. "These Centurions," the Empress said, "are not your true enemies."

"What?" Squint blurted out. "They abandoned me. Left me for dead. They kidnapped you and kept you captive."

"True and not true," she said. "It was them, but not completely them." Squint and Diamond looked at each other in disbelief and then down at Rock.

"Don't look at me," Rock said. "I'm just a bunch of rocks."

"Tell me," the Empress said. "Did you notice the dark scales forming on them?"

"Yes," Diamond said.

"That is an ancient magic," the Empress explained. "It found them and attached to them, like a virus. It fed off of them."

"It brings darkness," Squint said. "I found a scroll that said as much."

"Yes," the Empress said. "And slowly, very slowly, it began to control them, feeding off their hate, their fear, their jealousy. Adding to the darkness. And they were completely unaware, doing things they wouldn't normally have done."

"That's no excuse," Squint said.

"I think you're right," she said. "But did you notice your own neck and shoulders?" she asked, looking at his shoulder.

What did that mean? Squint glanced down and found scales. On him. "What?" he said. "How did they get there?"

"It fed off you. Your hate for those who wronged you," she said. "It brought darkness. And when you follow it, darkness grows. You have to shed it. Get rid of it."

"How?" Squint asked, looking at his own scales again.

"I will leave that to you to figure out," she said. "But now more darkness is coming. You all have made it strong."

She pointed out over the cliffs. A giant snake burst from the waves. It was the length of a wall around a large city and as thick as a castle. And it was covered in the same black scales.

As Squint gazed at the huge beast, his eyes glowed and his hands were tinged with light. "Can we defeat it?" he asked.

"We must face it," the Empress said. She looked down as the enormous serpent slithered across the top of the sea toward them.

Diamond covered herself in a completely impenetrable shield. Apparently, she had figured that out.

"We may need help," the Empress said. She reached out and touched Squint. His eyes blazed, he could feel the fire, the power. And then more.

Was the Empress giving him a new power? Or was this related to his own light? He didn't know, but he could see more. He could see farther. The serpent and beyond. And more. He could see through someone else's eyes. And those eyes were looking at him.

It was Diamond. He was looking through her eyes. And he could feel she knew it was worth it to side with him, to help the Empress. She was proud and strong. Yet scared. Scared to face another beast.

Then more light and Squint saw through someone else's eyes.

Gunn was awakening and Squint could see the world as he regained his footing. He felt the pull of the scales. Anger. Fear. Competition. Pressure. Everyone looking to him. It all surged through him.

Then Traz. The need to not back down. To show confidence. To not appear weak.

Then Lash. Then Madame Cool.

And then the Empress. Her eyes were different. Hers saw the good and the bad in everyone, yet tried to emphasize the good.

Squint gasped as he came back to his own eyes and the Empress let go.

"You must release your scales," the Empress said. "Then maybe you can help them release theirs. And then maybe, we may stand a chance."

"Okay," Squint said. "And I think it might be helpful to know how to blast light out of me. It was kind of a reaction last time."

She nodded. "Focus your mind, and will it through

your veins to blast it out your hands," she said. "You can do the same with your legs."

"And from my eyes?" I asked.

"It's the same idea," she said, "but it might help to squint."

—To be continued—

CHAPTER 37

SENT

"Get out of my way, pirate," Gavin said.

I was almost into the lunchroom and was beelining for my table.

"Pirates don't move for anyone," I said.

"My grandma walks faster than you," he said.

"Why don't you bring your grandma to school and we'll have a race," I said.

Gavin smiled and pushed me a little on the shoulder. It wasn't like we were friends now. Not even close. He really did mock people and push the limits too far. I'm sure he would make fun of me and mock my comics more. But there was a little piece of our old friendship there. Just a little.

"Hey," he said. "You guys weren't terrible in the assembly."

"That was like a week ago," I said.

"So?" he said.

"Thanks," I said. "I think."

I made my way to my table and pulled a new comic sheet out of my portfolio. It had another sketch of Squint and Rock looking out at the dark sea monster. I didn't have to squint. My eye had healed up well and the doctor had taken some of the stitches out. I could see just fine. Well, my left eye still wasn't the best, but I wasn't going to complain.

"I think I figured out why you're getting such a bad grade in science," McKell said, pointing at my comic pages after setting down her tray. "I saw you sketching again in class."

My grades hadn't healed as well as my eye.

"No way. I'm an expert multitasker," I said. I pulled out my peanut butter sandwich. I waited to eat at the table these days.

"Did you see how many hits our video had this morning?" she asked.

I nodded. "Like 20,000. Not bad." We had posted her song and it was doing well. Of course, the fact that Yellow tagged it as Danny's sister doing his challenge hadn't hurt. "And I think Danny would like that it's up for everyone to see."

McKell froze for a second. "I'm doing better at this not-caring-what-others-think thing, but try not to push it. It's freaking me out." She picked up her slice of pizza.

"So, I have something," I said, and lifted up an envelope that had already been opened once.

"What?" McKell asked. I slid it across the table. The top

left said "Grunger Comics," and their address. "Wait. No way." Her eyes got huge.

"Don't get your hopes up," I said. "I didn't win."

McKell's shoulders sagged. "Really? I'm sorry. Your comic is great, though," she said.

"It's atomic," I said. "Right?"

"That's right," she said and nodded big.

"But take a look," I said, and motioned for her to open the envelope. She looked confused but pulled it out and started in. After a minute she spoke up. "Wait," she said. "Is this guy like some famous comic-book guy writing to you?"

I nodded. "One of the best Grunger has."

"And he said," she started to read from the letter, "'Sorry you didn't win, Flint. But this has to be the best work I've seen from someone so young. You keep it up and you'll be working with people like me in no time.'" She got out of her seat and hugged me.

Maybe light was going to come shooting out of me like it did for Squint. In some ways, those three sentences were almost as good as a win. I was good. Gavin didn't know what he was talking about. I was on the right track.

McKell sat back down.

"Hey," a voice said. A girl with short blonde hair stood in front of our table.

McKell looked at her, then me. "Oh, this is Mila. She's new. I invited her to sit with us," she said.

I smiled as Mila laughed. "Flint invited me too," she

said. "I thought I was going to have to choose. I didn't know you two were friends." She set her stuff down and we started talking. I was just about to tell Mila that if she ever struggled in science that McKell could tutor her when my phone buzzed in my pocket. I looked at the incoming text.

> Hey Flinty. How's ur eye? I heard you had more problems. Do u still ♡ comic books? I'll bring you some.

Mom.

My cornea rejection scare had happened more than a week and a half ago. Why had she taken so long to ask? And do I still ♡ comics? If she was a good mom, there was no way she would even need to ask that question.

McKell was talking to Mila—and I needed to get back to them.

I started to put my phone away.

But my mom was reaching out to me. A week and a half late wasn't great, but at least she was trying.

Besides, she was my mom.

And for all I knew it was a pajama kind of day for her. Heck, maybe she was having a pajama kind of life.

For the first time in a very long time, I clicked *reply*.

> Hey, Mom. I'm okay. And I still love comics. My favorites are The Avengers.

And I sent it.

ACKNOWLEDGMENTS

Whenever a book comes out, there are a lot of people to thank. Let's start with you. Thank you for reading this book. We hope you enjoyed it. Feel free to look us up on social media and let us know what you thought. And if you liked it, feel free to spread the word. Thanks again.

Thanks to the teachers and librarians across the country who encourage their students to read. A special thanks to all of those who invited us to visit their schools. We loved it and we hoped your students did too. Keep up the compassion in action!

Thanks to all the bookstores across the nation who host our signings. We appreciate you giving us a venue to meet our readers.

Thanks to the great Shadow Mountain team. Thanks to Chris Schoebinger, Dave Brown, Heidi Taylor Gordon, and Lisa Mangum for loving the idea of Squint. Thanks to Chris and Heidi for reading several drafts and giving feedback to make it better. Thanks to Derk Koldewyn for his editorial eye. Thanks to Heather Ward for her fantastic cover. We love it! And thanks to Richard Erickson for his art direction, and Rachael Ward for formatting the book.

Thanks to our agent, Ben Grange, for loving this book and taking care of the business end of our careers so well. You're a rock star.

Thanks for all our awesome beta readers: Peggy Eddleman, Krista Isaacson, Shauna Holyoak, Rebecca Gage, Isaac Marble, Camille Smithson, and Amy Sandback.

Thanks to J. R. Simmons, Cody Cagle, Theresa Isidro, and Kaiya Liwanag for answering our questions about your experiences.

And thanks to all those who listened to Shelly's musicals and to Chad's parodies for years. Who knew we would use that rhyme and musicality to tell stories for kids one day?

And thanks to our five children for their patience and help while we write. Thanks for going to so many literary events. Thanks for letting us bounce ideas off you. Thanks for creating your own stories. And thanks for loving books.

DISCUSSION QUESTIONS

1. Flint loves to create comics. McKell loves to rhyme and write songs. What do you love to create? Why?
2. Flint felt nervous about others seeing his comics. McKell felt terrified to perform in front of others. Do you feel nervous when you show something you created to someone else? Why or why not? Do you think it's important to share what you create even if you feel nervous?
3. Flint loves comics and movies. What are some stories that you love?
4. Flint didn't feel like he had any friends at the beginning of the book. If someone at your school or in your neighborhood felt that way, what do you think you could do to help?

5. Flint was being raised by his grandparents. He didn't realize how hard they worked and sacrificed for him. Do you think we realize how much our parents and others work and sacrifice for us? Why or why not?

6. Danny had a rare disease called progeria, yet he had a positive attitude and tried to help others. Do you know anyone with an illness or difficulty who still has a positive attitude? Who? What impresses you about them?

7. If you were to start your own YouTube channel and give others challenges, what would you challenge them to do?

8. Even though Danny could edit his mistakes out of his videos, he didn't. Why is it okay sometimes to let others see our mistakes?

9. When Danny died, everyone in his family dealt with the sadness differently. Have you ever had anyone die that you were close to? How did you deal with the sadness? Was there anything that other people around you could do that would have helped?

10. McKell's mom stayed in her pajamas when she was having a really hard day. Do you ever have really hard days? What did you do to get through your hard days? What could you do to help others during their hard days?

11. Flint and McKell became friends and helped each other out throughout the story. Who are your friends? How do they help you? How do you help them?